MYSTIC SPIRES POST-MORTEM

STACEY JERNIGAN

MYSTIC SPIRES POST-MORTEM

A COLD-CASE LEGAL THRILLER

BROWN BOOKS
PUBLISHING GROUP

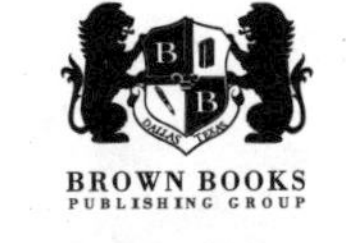

Mystic Spires Post-Mortem: A Cold-Case Legal Thriller

Brown Books Publishing Group
Dallas, TX/New York, NY
www.BrownBooks.com
(972) 381-0009

A New Era in Publishing®

Publisher's Cataloging-In-Publication Data

A New Era in Publishing®
Publisher's Cataloging-In-Publication Data
Names: Jernigan, Stacey, author.
Title: Mystic Spires post-mortem : a cold-case legal thriller / Stacey Jernigan.
Description: Dallas, TX ; New York, NY : Brown Books Publishing Group, [2025]
Identifiers: LCCN: 2025936829 | ISBN: 9781612547251 (paperback) | 9781612547268 (ePub)
Subjects: LCSH: Women judges--Texas--Fiction. | Murder--Investigation--Texas--Fiction. | Heiresses--Death--Fiction. | Cold cases (Criminal investigation)--Texas--Fiction. | Deception--Fiction. | Corruption--Fiction. | Dallas (Tex.)--Fiction. | LCGFT: Legal fiction (Literature) | Detective and mystery fiction. | BISAC: FICTION / Mystery & Detective. | FICTION / Crime. | FICTION / Legal.
Classification: LCC: PS3610.E733 M97 2025 | DDC: 813/.6--dc23

ISBN 978-1-61254-725-1
EISBN 978-1-61254-726-8
LCCN 2025936829

Printed in Canada
10 9 8 7 6 5 4 3 2 1

For more information or to contact the author, please go to www.SJNovels.com.

AUTHOR'S NOTE

Because I am a sitting United States judge, and I am also married to a retired law enforcement officer, I feel compelled, at the outset, to clarify certain points regarding this novel.

The following is a work of fiction. While some of the characters and events may be loosely based on actual persons and events—including an unsolved murder from the 1980s near Dallas, Texas, and various other Texas legal folklore—the human characters in this novel are absolutely fictional. Judge Avery Lassiter, the main character in this novel, is not me.

Second, one should not assume that any statement or opinion expressed or implied by any characters in this novel are necessarily mine or are somehow a reflection on how I might rule on any particular issue in any case in the future.

Dedicated to my many hardworking and enthusiastic law clerks and interns over the years, who have not only been a tremendous help to me and the parties appearing in our court but have selflessly deferred more lucrative career opportunities in the name of public service. I hope that they will always passionately pursue justice and the rule of law and will see a bit of each of him or herself in the law clerk characters in this book.

The dead cannot cry out for justice.
It is a duty of the living to do so for them.
—Lois McMaster Bujold

ACKNOWLEDGMENTS

I want to start by thanking the publishing team at Brown Books for having confidence in this novel and helping make it a much better product than I could have otherwise achieved. They have been consummate professionals. They have also been patient and understanding with the fact that my "day job" and first commitment is being a judge for the public. Second, I want to thank my spouse, whose experience as a law enforcement officer has given me more than a few ideas for my writing. He is not "Max Lassiter," but there are plenty of parallels, to be sure.

1

THE DEATH OF GENEVIEVE MESERO

DECEMBER 29, 2016

Genevieve Mesero, affectionately known as "Gigi" to some, was pronounced dead by the Dallas County Medical Examiner's office at 2:42 a.m. on December 29, 2016. Her beautiful, lifeless body was poised gracefully on her barely tousled king-sized bed inside her massive penthouse suite at the Mystic Spires Hotel. Yet another tragedy at the enigmatic establishment.

Gigi's body was found by her sister Valentina and Valentina's husband, Cort Daniel. When emergency personnel arrived on the scene—moments after the pair discovered her—Valentina appeared almost catatonic, shaking and seemingly unable to speak. According to Cort's statements given to the Dallas Police, Valentina and Cort had rushed the ten miles from their house in University Park to Gigi's penthouse at the Mystic Spires. Valentina had received a panicky phone call from her sister saying she was having trouble breathing and felt very ill. It wasn't clear why Gigi had called Valentina and not 911 or even the hotel front desk. It was equally unclear why Valentina and Cort had not immediately called 911 themselves and chosen instead to first make the drive to check on Gigi. At least thirty minutes of potentially critical time was lost before getting medical help to Gigi.

When EMTs and police first laid eyes on Genevieve, they were not quite sure what they were seeing: a death by natural causes or something sinister. Gigi was lying on her back, wearing blue silk pajamas, and her brown eyes were open and staring blankly at the ceiling. There were no signs of any bodily trauma. Rigor mortis had not yet set in, although the muscles of her face were stiff. There were no signs of foul play or an accident. The doors to Gigi's balcony overlooking Dallas's skyline were ajar, allowing in a chilly breeze, and there were two empty glasses on an outdoor table along with a bottle of cava in an ice bucket. Other than that, there were no signs of anyone else having been on the premises. As if that were not all unsettling enough, a Bose speaker was blaring, playing one song over and over again: Van Morrison's "Brown Eyed Girl."

Gigi was a well-known, thirty-nine-year-old Texas socialite, the daughter of the late Guillermo Mesero, a legendary Mexican American business titan, and his spirited French wife Vivienne, who, ironically, died tragically at the same young age as Gigi now had. Gigi was divorced, childless, and lived alone. She and her sister had inherited a rather sizable fortune a couple of years earlier when their father died.

It would be several weeks until an autopsy revealed that Genevieve Mesero's death was caused by strychnine poison contained in a bottle of NyQuil cold medicine found inside a drawer in a table next to her bed. She took NyQuil frequently to help her dose off to sleep.

Was it suicide or a homicide? Genevieve had a complicated life. The very rich often do.

It did not take long for police cars, forensics teams, and media helicopters to overtake the scene at the Mystic Spires Hotel.

Judge Avery Lassiter, who was awake in the wee hours watching holiday movies, wondered why her husband, Max, a police officer who was working the dreaded third watch (4 p.m. to midnight), was not home by now. She was surprised he had not checked in. It was several hours after his shift should have ended. That was rarely a good sign.

Avery decided to phone Max. After several rings, he picked up.

"Hey, babe."

Avery could hear loud rap music playing in the background: Coolio's "Gangsta's Paradise." Really? Where was he?

"Max? I've been kind of worried. Where are you? Sounds like a nightclub or something."

"Oh, yeah, right, Avery." Max snickered. "Actually, most of the nightclubs are closed at this hour. The hardcore club crowd has moved on to after-hour parties in vacant parking lots. That's where things get really interesting."

"I don't know what you mean by really interesting."

"You don't want to know. Trust me. Anyway, that's Joe Meno's annoying music. We're all back at the station. He calls it his 'keep everyone awake because we've got work to do' playlist. He only plays rap music on odd-number calendar days. He plays country or rock the other nights of the week."

"Okay, fine. Are you going to be home anytime soon?"

"Uh, afraid not. I'm doing some intel work right now that can't wait."

"Intel work at four a.m.?"

"Yep. You know that hotel heiress, Genevieve Mesero, who keeps having fires and other weird things happen at that downtown hotel?"

"The Mystic Spires?"

"Yep. She was found dead there a couple of hours ago under suspicious circumstances."

"Oh my God. You're kidding! That's horrible, Max!"

"Yeah, it's horrible," Max replied, not sounding particularly horrified. But that was the life of a homicide detective. "Anyway, I'm looking through some video footage from some nearby cameras and doing some license plate scans and stuff."

"This is so sad. She is so young and beautiful. And here we go again with our worlds colliding, Max."

"Was. What's that supposed to mean?"

"Genevieve filed a personal bankruptcy case in my court a few years ago. She had a lot of problems, as I recall."

"Oh yeah, you told me." Max took a sip of something, probably coffee, and slurped a little. He must be pretty tired, Avery thought. He usually was a very careful, almost dainty drinker. "I'll never understand how massively wealthy people can just wake up one day and say, 'Times have gotten hard. I think I'll declare bankruptcy.' I thought a person had to be broke. But, yeah, I do remember . . . something about a big lawsuit and wanting to keep her penthouse."

"And the banks weren't having any of it," said Avery.

"Bankruptcy. Crazy laws."

"Her lawyers were arguing in my courtroom about that for days. Oh my God! Max, is that where she was found dead—up in her penthouse?"

"Yeah. And I have to tell you, Avery. It's an amazing place with a beautiful view. I can see why she wanted to keep it. You can even see your courthouse from it."

"Well, I'm sure there are much prettier views to be seen from it than our sad, old building. Gosh, it's just so tragic, Max. Genevieve took the witness stand several times. I thought she was absolutely lovely—even though her life seemed a total mess, at least financially. She seemed shy and scared. Had these big, brown, kind eyes. And you know she has a beautiful sister, too. Her name is Valentina."

"Yep, that's her name."

"I'm surprised, Max. I didn't think you kept up with the fete set in Dallas."

Max did not respond. Avery could hear his computer keyboard clicking rapidly, almost in rhythm with the annoying rap music still playing in the background.

"You know, I actually once saw the two of them," Avery remembered, "the two sisters—traveling together in Valencia, Spain, a few years ago. Ironically, it was when I was with my sister Suzanne on spring break."

"You what? You and your sister saw the two of them?"

"It was just one of those random things. But good grief. This is just so disturbing. How did she die? Was it murder? You just said, 'dead under suspicious circumstances.'"

"All I can tell you is her sister and her brother-in-law were the ones who found her and called 911. I'll tell you more details when it's public. I imagine it will be soon enough with all the news reporters snooping around at the scene."

"God, that hotel is starting to seem absolutely cursed. Do you remember that there was a young man who fell, or jumped, or maybe was pushed, off a balcony a while back? There've been multiple weird things happening there. Fires. I can't even remember how many now—maybe three?"

"Okay, Avery. I've really got to go. I hope I'll be home before sunrise, but you know how it is."

"All right. I'll let you get back to your intel work. Love you."

"Love you, too. Good night, or morning, or whatever it is now."

"Probably should say 'morning.' Bye."

Avery turned off her lamp but didn't turn off her TV or put down her phone.

Avery's first memory of the Mystic Spires dated back to when she was a small child growing up in Dallas. Every year, her mother would dress her and her sister Suzanne up in their best clothes and take them to the annual Neiman Marcus "Fortnight" event that occurred every fall at the downtown store location. Afterwards, they would visit the Mystic Spires for high tea. It was called the Estrella Mansion back then. Avery smiled. Her family wasn't rich, but it was her mother's way of exposing her daughters to culture. The Fortnights were launched a few weeks before the winter holidays. Avery had been sad when the store stopped doing them. Each year the store would transform itself to look like some foreign country—France, Italy, England, Germany, Austria. There would be exquisite products—food and fashion—from these countries. Sometimes celebrities like Coco Chanel or Sophia Loren would attend. There would be galas and ceremonies. Beautiful art and photographs. Magnificent and theatrical displays. There was even a live bull in the china shop one year for the Spain Fortnight. It was such a magical way to learn about foreign countries back in a time when travel was expensive and more difficult. For a middle-class kid living in Dallas back in the '70s and '80s, it was a way to explore the world.

There was no way she was getting back to sleep now. She decided to Google the Mystic Spires Hotel to refresh her memory about its various scandals and tragedies. Maybe she could somehow be of help to Max, though she doubted it.

The Mystic Spires. Originally known as the Estrella Mansion. It was a charming luxury hotel that had recently been designated as a Texas Historic Landmark. It was constructed in 1894—not quite fifty years after Texas became a state in the U.S. It was one of the oldest big buildings in Dallas. The property had been through several name changes over the decades, with the wealthy Mesero family changing it to Mystic Spires when they acquired it in the year 1994 on its hundred-year anniversary. There had been much fanfare at the time they purchased and renamed it. The family patriarch, Guillermo Mesero, was an immigrant to Dallas from Mexico City. He had made a fortune there working with Carlos Slim's conglomerate, Grupo Carso, before moving to Texas. He was married to a beautiful French English woman named Vivienne Crane, who died in a plane crash when Gigi and her sister were small children. The hotel had hosted the rich and famous and even presidents over the years. It was sixteen stories tall and was built in the Spanish Colonial Revival style, with a white stucco exterior and red tile roof surrounded by elaborated parapets. It had grand spiral staircases and a red-carpet entrance. It had expensive artwork throughout and chandeliers imported from Italy. Its woodwork and wainscoted walls were exquisite. Every room was unique. There were pictures of famous guests and other visitors from over the years displayed in the lobby: Teddy Roosevelt, Frank Sinatra, Mick Jagger, Oprah, various Mexican and South American presidents. The hotel had a basement that was once used as a speakeasy during Prohibition, with a tunnel that led to some nearby horse stables through which drunk gambling men ran from police when it was raided—an occasional event. It had a lovely city park across from it which the Dallas Historical Society and Dallas Junior League had maintained for years. Gigi, with her father's blessing, arranged for these volunteer groups to plant mystic spires all over the park—the sturdy, bluish-purple flower that she had loved so much since she was a child. There were also mystic spires flowers all around the hotel property. According to nearly every single review, the inside of the hotel smelled "absolutely heavenly."

I'm never getting back to sleep after reading this, Avery thought.

Gigi's sister was the one who found her. Avery thought of her own sister, Suzanne, and how devastated she would be if anything bad happened to her. She started to text Suzanne, then thought better of it. She was sure Suzanne would remember seeing Gigi and her sister in Spain. She'd check later.

Avery put her phone down and turned her TV volume back up and started watching the old movie *White Christmas* for a while. In the scene, Rosemary Clooney and the petite, lesser-known actress who played Clooney's sister (whose name Avery could not remember) were singing their "Sisters" duet with their big feather fans and boas. Irony?

Genevieve Mesero's death-by-poison would remain an unsolved mystery—eventually the proverbial "cold case"—much to the anguish of friends, family, and law enforcement officers who put in enormous amounts of time and energy trying to find answers. It was almost universally considered to have been a murder, not suicide (although some people would long have their doubts). Suspects included Gigi's sister, Valentina, Valentina's husband, Cort, an investment banker named Blake Martin whom Genevieve dated in recent months, as well as Gigi's ex-husband, who was a former personal injury lawyer turned lobbyist who once garishly advertised himself as the "Flamethrower." More dark-horse candidates for murderer included Genevieve's horse trainer's wife and a hotel groundskeeper living on-site in a trailer.

2

ALDO MOSES, THE MYSTIC SPIRES GROUNDSKEEPER

Aldo Moses was a skinny, worn-out Caucasian man who was a regular fixture around the Mystic Spires Hotel. He had bloodshot, bulging blue eyes, thinning red hair that he usually pulled back in a ponytail, and a scraggly gray goatee. He had fading green tattoos covering both of his arms. He stood and walked somewhat hunched over. Other workers at the property cruelly referred to him as "The Walking C" behind his back. He generally had a Marlboro cigarette hanging from his mouth or fingers. He looked much older than his forty-two years. "Meth will do that to you," Max Lassiter would often say to his kids.

Aldo Moses had come to the Mystic Spires through Cort Daniel, Valentina's husband. Aldo had worked for a landscaping company that Cort once owned before Cort married Valentina. Cort had "married up," to be sure, when he wedded Valentina and chose to cease most of his previous, money-losing business endeavors at that time. He slowly took on more involvement managing the hotel property. When Gigi and Valentina decided they needed someone full-time at the property to keep the grounds and also work as a handyman, Cort recommended Aldo. Aldo stayed in an old RV trailer in a wooded area behind the Mystic Spires. He was quiet and very reliable generally, although he did have a few blips on his record. He had once served time for petty theft and several BMVs (burglaries of motor vehicles). He also worked at a big-cat conservatory in Oklahoma whose owner—an unusual man of much notoriety due to a reality TV show—was convicted of animal cruelty.

Those murky days were all behind Aldo. He enjoyed the more quiet, stable existence he lived now. He could regularly be seen driving around the property in his golf cart, stopping frequently to pull weeds, collect debris, and inspect equipment and sprinkler heads and the like. He had indoor duties as well since something was always breaking in a hotel over a hundred years old.

On the night of Gigi Mesero's death, Aldo Moses was not on duty but passed out in his trailer after a combination of one too many joints and Busch Natty Light beers.

Officers Max Lassiter and Joe Meno were wrapping up their duties as Dallas PD covert officers early on the morning of December 29, 2016. They had stayed well past midnight after a sting operation the FBI brought them in on involving some Colombian jewelry thieves. As they were starting to leave their duty station, a homicide detective put out a call asking for available officers to come down to the Mystic Spires Hotel and help with canvassing the perimeter of the property. Max and Meno quickly volunteered. They put on their patrol uniforms and other equipment and were out the door in five minutes. This was the life of a police officer. Tedium, mixed with occasional terror. Or tragedy. It was unclear what this assignment would be.

Shortly after their arrival at the Mystic Spires, Officers Max Lassiter and Joe Meno were walking the grounds, looking primarily for the locations of video cameras. They were having amazingly bad luck. They were finding very few cameras, and none so far seemed to be operational. The young man working at the front desk that night was a fairly new employee, and he was of no help whatsoever regarding where cameras were located and which ones worked. He suggested that they ask the groundskeeper and handyman, Aldo Moses, who would probably be in his trailer east of the property.

When Max and Meno happened upon the old aluminum trailer that the desk man had described, they could hear Johnny Cash playing inside and noticed the faint, unmistakable smell of weed.

"Hmmm. What do you think the chances are that this fella answers when we knock?" Meno asked Max.

"Well, considering that none of the sirens or lights seem to have roused him, I'd say he's out cold."

"He could have a gun."

"Oh, I'd bet money on that, Meno. How long have you lived in Texas?"

"Seriously, knock, but I'm just saying be prepared for anything."

"I always am, Meno. Always am. Just call me a Boy Scout."

Max knocked on the weathered trailer door. No answer. He knocked several more times. Still no answer.

Finally, Max started announcing himself. "Aldo Moses. This is Dallas Police. We'd like to talk to you."

Nothing.

"Shit. What now?"

"Let's just wait a few more minutes."

"You think we have probable cause to jiggle the door handle? Just go on in?"

"How long have you been doing this, Meno?"

"Longer than you, smart-ass. But you were the one who talked to Detective Stone about this. I don't know if there are exigent circumstances or if anyone's got a warrant or consent or anything."

At that point, Aldo Moses abruptly opened his door, squinting his eyes and coughing profusely. "What the hell's going on out here?"

"Hello, Mr. Moses," Max began. "We're Officers Lassiter and Meno. There's been an incident up at the property, and we are hoping to get some video camera footage. Can you help us? The front desk bellman suggested we try you."

"What kind of an incident?" Moses's words were slurred, and he reeked of beer and, expectedly, marijuana.

"We can't really say, sir. We're not the ones in charge of this investigation and didn't even respond to the 911 call. We're just helping out the investigating team, mostly here on the outside of the property."

"Well, I would need Ms. Mesero's permission before I do anything. Not giving you anything just because that little kid in diapers at the front desk told you to check with me."

Max and Meno hesitated.

"Well, are you willing to come up to the hotel lobby with us, and we will check with the detective in charge and see if we have consent or a warrant?"

"I guess so. But I'll tell you right now, the cameras around here are out half the time. They're old, and the security company that is supposed to monitor them for us is terrible. Don't know what you're going to be able to pull up from them. Let me put a shirt and shoes on."

"Go ahead, sir."

Max and Meno looked at each other, and then both craned their heads as Aldo Moses walked back inside the trailer, leaving the door wide open behind him. They were making sure he didn't grab a weapon or make a so-called "furtive move," but, of course, they were also trying to see if there was anything in plain sight that might be interesting.

Nothing noticeable. Just a rather filthy trailer. Of course, they didn't even know what they should be looking for at this juncture. The music finally stopped just as Cash remembered how his mother told him never to play with guns.

Aldo Moses walked out after a few moments, now dressed in a work shirt with the Mystic Spires logo on it, along with blue jeans and work boots. Max noticed that the work boots looked very clean, almost shiny. Cops are always picking up on these kinds of details.

"Let's go, Officers." Aldo pointed to a stone path that led to the hotel entrance. "This is my shortcut."

Max and Meno followed him. If Aldo Moses had done anything wrong, they were not getting any visible hints of it. He seemed annoyed and curious more than anything else.

3

SCHADENFREUDE AS A LEGAL STRATEGY

2018, TWO YEARS LATER

"What are you looking at, Judge?"

Judge Avery Lassiter's two law clerks, Millicent and Tom, eagerly popped into her office one morning shortly before the start of a messy trial they had scheduled. Judge Lassiter was staring pensively out of her fourteenth-floor window, going back and forth from her binoculars to her Tiffany blue eyeglasses.

"You're not going to believe this. I don't believe this. This is absolutely surreal."

"What, Judge?" Millicent asked as she and her colleague rushed to the window. Even at their relatively young age, they had learned to never take anything lightly at the courthouse. An "unbelievable" event could, frankly, be anything. It was ceaseless chaotic activity at this place.

"Oh, I'm just watching the Mystic Spires Hotel burn. Again. It keeps happening. I mean fires at the property. I think this is the fourth time now that the hotel has caught fire. I hope this time it's not a goner. But it's engulfed all over. That hotel is such an elegant, old jewel. So much history. I just can't believe what I'm seeing."

Millicent and Tom put their faces almost against the glass and watched the distant flames and dark plumes of smoke. Fire trucks were rushing toward the property, sirens blaring. Police cars and ambulances weren't far behind. Helicopters were swirling.

"Wow. I think it is definitely a goner," Tom remarked.

"I've never heard anything about that old hotel," Millicent admitted. "I've just never paid that much attention to it. I wonder if it was arson."

"Oh, aren't you cute, Milly. Already thinking like a lawyer." Judge Lassiter smirked. "Let's just hope everyone got out of there alive."

The three of them continued to stare in silence at the raging inferno. Avery finally put her binoculars down. They had been a gift from a former law clerk who liked to gaze out the courthouse windows during the workday—a little too much, perhaps.

"This is just mind-boggling. It's as if that hotel has been cursed for decades. There have been so many tragedies there. Mysterious deaths. Scandals. A veritable palace of intrigue, one might say. One of the two sisters who owned it—or who inherited it, actually—died a couple of years ago of strychnine poisoning. Genevieve Mesero. Do y'all remember that?"

Tom and Millicent shrugged their shoulders and shook their heads.

"I guess you were studying too hard in law school at the time to pay attention to the news reports. The police have never solved her murder—some are not even willing to concede that it *was* a murder, really. Although I think the evidence was pretty convincing that it was, ultimately. Anyway, she filed a personal bankruptcy case here in our court a couple of years before that. It was crazy. She tried to legally shield her huge penthouse at the hotel and its contents as her protected homestead. It was legal Armageddon as far as her bank creditors were concerned."

"We've seen that legal playbook a few times, haven't we, Judge?"

"Yep. More than a few. It's really not that unique of a strategy anymore, is it? It's even been done by other folks over the years at that very same property. What's that expression? A man's—or woman's—home is his or her castle? Why shouldn't that apply to a ten-million-dollar penthouse overlooking Downtown Dallas?"

"Sometimes I cannot tell when you are being serious or sarcastic, Judge!"

"I think the same thing about the two of you." Avery smiled.

"Oh my God, Judge. Do you think that one of her creditors was mad enough to kill her over that legal maneuver?"

"Oh my goodness, Millicent. Surely not. I mean, I doubt it. I suppose it's possible. According to the news reports and true crime podcasts, there was a long list of suspects in her murder investigation, but I don't think her friendly hometown bankers were among them."

"Judge, it feels like things keep burning all over around here. It was just recently that we walked in on you watching Big Tex go up in flames over at the State Fair. That was pretty creepy, looking at his fifty-foot-tall fried skeleton after it'd been burned to a crisp."

"And right about the same time, there was that old church that caught fire over by the homeless shelter," Tom put in.

"Yes," Avery said. "We have a bird's-eye view of disasters up here on the high floors of the courthouse, don't we?"

"Kind of feels like a metaphor for what we do around here," said Millicent. "Disasters are us. Fires outside and fires inside our courtroom. Big fires. Dumpster fires."

Tom rolled his eyes at Millicent. "Someone's getting a little melodramatic, don't you think?"

"Come on, Tom. Play along. This is the part where you start quoting Alfred from Batman. You know, 'Some men just want to watch the world burn.' Your favorite quote." Millicent grinned.

"Speaking of fires in our courtroom, where's my research for today, Millicent?"

Millicent handed Avery a stack of research. "Here it is. And here is a sur-reply filed by the defendant at eleven fifty-nine p.m. last night."

"Aw, how nice of them to get it filed before midnight. I feel so guilty, though, that I was not waiting up for it."

"Judge, I think you will say that it reads like one of my classic 'Milly Vanilli' work products I hand to you now and again. It says the same thing over and over—but just because it's long doesn't make it good."

Avery smiled. "God, I love that one. A law clerk a few years ago came up with that line and it is still great, even if fewer and fewer people get the reference these days."

Tom chimed in. “I think you’ve got plenty of time to read it, Judge. I bet some of the lawyers are going to be late today. There are a bunch of protesters outside on the other side of the building, across Commerce Street. It was almost impossible getting in on that side of the building.”

“Hmm. Wonder what they’re protesting today?” Avery asked.

Tom replied, “Lack of everything.”

Avery looked at Tom strangely.

“Sarcasm or serious?”

Tom spoke further. “Actually, it just sounded like the usual shrill anti-corporate rhetoric we hear out there every so often when there is no current political or social injustice scandal for the protestors to complain about.”

Millicent interrupted. “Were there any of those ‘The Birds Aren’t Real’ people out there today? I just love those kooks.”

“I don’t know. There were probably some of them intermixed in the crowd somewhere. But I know at least one of the lawyers won’t be late. Hardcore Hank. I saw Hank Atkins hurriedly weaving his way through the crowd of protesters when I came in. One of the protesters—a guy wearing one of those *V for Vendetta* masks—bumped into him with a sign that said, ‘Stop Corporate Greed,’ and Hank screamed, ‘Get the hell out of my way. I’m a lawyer and I will bleed you.’”

Avery replied, “That sounds about right.”

Tom continued. “Then I see Hardcore Hank downstairs at the security check-in a few minutes later. He screams at one of the court security officers for allegedly being rude to him. He says, ‘Why don’t you go to work at Walmart part-time, buddy, so you can take their greeter training course and learn some people skills.’”

“Good grief!” Millicent exclaimed. “What an asshole.”

Avery winced. “Careful with the name-calling. Although it’s probably one hundred percent accurate.”

“I think this is just the way Hank pre-games for a trial. Bark at every human being who crosses his path on the way in. It’s like a warm-up routine.” Tom grinned and sipped his coffee.

“I suspect Hank’s probably still angry at the security officers over the time they took his gun away a couple of years ago. He said he happened to forget about his Glock semiautomatic handgun that was in his briefcase.

He actually accused the security officers of performing a cavity search on him after that. His usual hyperbole. You all should probably nickname him Hyperbole Hank instead of Hardcore Hank."

"Good one, Judge!"

Avery tried to redirect the conversation. "Okay. Let's talk about the trial now. Millicent, tell me about these cases you brought me and the Milly Vanilli midnight brief. Tom, why don't you go out in the courtroom and see who's there and who's running late."

"You got it." Tom scurried off.

An enjoyable, disgraceful spectacle. That's what this trial promised to be, based on pre-trial skirmishes. It was Hardcore Hank versus the Baby-Faced Assassin. Well, at least those were the two nicknames chosen by Judge Lassiter's adorably irreverent law clerks to describe the two lead lawyers. They were the kind of lawyers who woke up every morning and said, "Who am I going to sue today?" Suing people was not simply a way to pay the bills. It was their whole raison d'être. They were natural-born killers. A win in court wasn't truly a win unless the other side died a slow and painful death. It was what Judge Lassiter called "schadenfreude as a legal strategy." The more the other side suffered, the happier each of the adversaries was. Lawyer provocateurs.

Judge Lassiter told her clerks that this case reminded her of something Walt Disney once famously said. "Disneyland will never be completed. It will continue to grow as long as there is imagination left in the world." Neither would this case, apparently. It might never be finished as long as these lawyers kept imagining new arguments and strategies. They had boundless creativity. But not in a good way. They had been litigating for years now. First in state court and now in Avery's court.

As Judge Lassiter scanned through the stack of cases Millicent had brought her, Tom rejoined them.

"Everyone is present in the courtroom and ready, Judge. I heard the Baby-Faced Assassin ask Hardcore Hank if he wanted to go out in the attorney conference room and see if they could hammer out a few stipulations on evidence to save the court and everyone time, and Hardcore Hank replied, 'I wouldn't vomit in the same room as you, kid.'"

"Hank said *what*? What does that even mean?" Millicent shrieked.

Avery poured herself more coffee. "Good grief. I don't know what that means. I guess that's Hank's way of trash-talking before the big competition."

"Oh, and I think Hank's new young associate Benjamin's middle name must be 'Goddammit,' because Hank kept saying 'Benjamin Goddammit!', like fourteen times."

Avery sighed. "Hank clearly needs therapy."

"Yep," Millicent replied. "I have often said that lawyers need their own section in the *DSM*. A special section focusing on personality disorders in the lawyer population. Narcissism would be a biggie. But it runs much deeper. Sometimes I swear a lot of lawyers are sociopaths. Hardcore Hank being a prime example." Millicent had been a psychology major in college.

"Ouch, Milly. A little cynical, don't you think? Lawyers are not all a bad lot. There are many more good ones than bad ones! But Hank does fall on the spectrum for something. None of us are qualified to say. Not even you, my dear smart Milly. Anyway, gird your loins. It's time to go into court."

Avery went to her closet to grab her robe.

"All, rise. This court is now in session. The Honorable Avery Lassiter presiding." David, the courtroom deputy, had a loud, deep voice that boomed throughout the space. It was intimidating as hell, and Avery kind of liked that.

"Good morning. Please be seated."

Avery glanced around at the lawyers as she walked into the courtroom and sat down behind her bench. There was a PowerPoint already up on the courtroom video monitors that looked like it was in 4-point font. That would be useful.

The Baby-Faced Assassin made the sign of the cross as Avery sat down in her cushy chair. Was that a genuine act of faith on his part at this moment? Or was that an indication that he was about to hurl one of his famous legal Hail Marys? The action made Avery feel uncomfortable. It kind of reminded her of the time Max had arrested a notorious gangbanger who frequently posted pictures of himself on social media. In the photos, the guy would be coming out of Mass with his grandmother just before going out to commit some heinous crime. The caption: "Praying before hitting a lick."

Hardcore Hank was fussing at his associate Benjamin under his breath. Maybe Benjamin was the one who chose the 4-point font for the PowerPoint, earning him his new nickname.

There was a small crowd in the courtroom and a few lawyers on the Zoom video screen.

Kyle Darby, the Baby-Faced Assassin, was plaintiff's counsel. He was probably in his late thirties, but he looked twelve. His abilities were certainly not those of a novice. He was always exceedingly prepared and was a wicked cross-examiner. He had obviously paid attention to that cardinal rule of former Texas lawyer and secretary of state James Baker about the "Five P's": Proper Preparation Prevents Poor Performance. His opening statements and closing arguments were always perfect. They were the verbal equivalent of astronaut food—small bits of information that conveyed just what he needed to say and nothing more. Every statement was like a concise but informative Hemingway sentence. And he was a sharp dresser, too. Expensive, well-tailored suits with Hermès ties. While he was baby-faced, his demeanor was not one of innocence. He always wore a mean game face (even when making the sign of the cross, come to think of it). Today, to Avery's surprise, his wavy brown hair was pulled back in a man bun. Millicent would, no doubt, be talking about Kyle Darby's new man bun for days.

Kyle Darby's client, Ed Frankel, had a rather milquetoast comportment. But, apparently, he had a reputation as a brilliant financial advisor. He believed that he had been cheated out of fees and commissions from his former employer, a large consulting firm. What might have been a simple breach-of-contract lawsuit had morphed into an epic legal battle. His former employer, Cronus Consulting, countered back with claims against Frankel of fraud, defamation, theft of business, breach of fiduciary duties, and assorted other causes of action.

Hardcore Hank was counsel for the defendant Cronus Consulting. Hank was in his sixties, with a gray crew cut, thin and fit. He had large, bulging brown eyes that he seemed proud to brandish like weapons—frequently taking his glasses off at dramatic moments in court and glaring at a witness or his adversary. It was as if his eyes and glasses were props in a theatrical performance. Hank wore nothing but gray suits and, oddly, gray ties. Avery told her clerks that maybe this was because his favorite color seemed to be "morally gray"—he was always traversing dubious legal zones. Folklore around town (started by Hank's former associate, whose middle name might also have been "Goddammit") was that Hank had a tattoo of a serpent winding around his right arm. It was hard to separate fact from fiction when it came to Hardcore Hank—both inside and outside the courtroom. But what was clear was that Hank viewed himself as a hammer and everyone else as a nail. He, in combination with the egomaniacal client representatives at Cronus Consulting, presented a dangerous team. Obliteration of Ed Frankel appeared to be their singular goal. Their Rambo litigation tactics had eventually driven Frankel into the bittersweet sanctuary of bankruptcy. But the legal battle was far from over. Neither party was remotely close to laying down arms and calling it a day.

Avery began. "Good morning, counsel. Before we get started with opening statements, do we have any stipulations to announce or other housekeeping matters?"

Hardcore Hank stood up and approached the lawyer lectern.

"Good morning, Judge. It is with great regret that I am asking for a continuance today."

The Baby-Faced Assassin sprang to his feet.

"Your Honor! He has got to be kidding. This is outrageous! I've heard nothing about this! In fact, I tried to talk to Mr. Atkins this morning about stipulations, and he refused to even have a conversation with me!"

Tom whispered to Millicent, "I'm surprised he left out the part about Hank telling him he wouldn't vomit in the same room with him."

Avery's face did not hide her irritation. "Mr. Atkins, I'm sure you've got a good explanation for this. Why on earth are you asking for a continuance on the morning of trial? I'm not very happy considering I have spent the last couple of days reading your various motions to exclude evidence and the extensive case authority you cited."

"Your Honor, I do, indeed, have a very good explanation. There is an important witness that we have been trying to locate for several months. The witness has finally surfaced and the information the witness has about Mr. Frankel is explosive."

"Is Mr. Atkins going to share the identity of this mystery witness or are we going to have to sit here with bated breath while he keeps us in suspense?"

"Well, Mr. Atkins?" Avery grabbed for her Texas Longhorns coffee mug.

"The witness is Darla Frankel, Mr. Frankel's ex-wife."

Mr. Frankel suddenly looked as though all the blood had drained from his face.

Naturally, the Baby-Faced Assassin expressed complete outrage. "Judge, this is so preposterous it is likely sanctionable. What possible relevant and unbiased testimony could Mr. Frankel's ex-wife provide in this lawsuit? She's never been listed in any Rule 26 disclosures as a person with knowledge of the disputes. Mr. Atkins has never said anything about wanting her testimony or trying to locate her. Here we go again with Mr. Atkins's outlandish delay tactics. I urge you to sanction him and order this trial to begin now!"

Avery paused. "Mr. Atkins, let's hear why you think this is relevant. And assuming it is, why you allegedly couldn't find the witness until recently."

"Judge, Ms. Frankel lives in Costa Rica. She moved there about two years ago—shortly after her divorce from the plaintiff became final. She was married to the plaintiff until shortly after my client fired him. She knows a lot about what happened between Mr. Frankel and my client. Mr. Frankel basically paid her off in the divorce settlement to buy her silence, bought her a property in Costa Rica, and told her to stay there or he'd ruin her life."

"Objection, Your Honor. This is insanity. He's making this up as he goes." The Baby-Faced Assassin was being ambushed, and he didn't like it.

Avery interjected. "Mr. Atkins, this sounds rather far-fetched. Like you might be bringing domestic dirty laundry into a business dispute."

"Judge, Ms. Frankel knows a lot. A whole lot, and it's disturbing. Highly disturbing. For one thing, in the divorce property settlement, the subject of this lawsuit against Cronus Consulting came up, and Mr. Frankel valued it at zero dollars for the purposes of the division of the marital estate. And yet now Mr. Frankel is asking for one hundred million dollars in damages from my client. Second, Ms. Frankel has knowledge about her ex-husband stealing proprietary business information from my client—things like client data, business development strategies, and certain specialized software that performs financial analyses. She said she has overheard things and even took pictures and made recordings of his phone calls—just in case she ever needed it during their divorce case. Now she wants to share what she knows.

She has been in and out of rehab and basically off the grid in Costa Rica the past two years, but we finally tracked her down in Costa Rica. It wasn't easy. We were very diligent. My client and I believe it would be a grave miscarriage of justice if we didn't have an opportunity to depose this witness and present her testimony."

"Judge, this is beyond the pale, even for Mr. Atkins. I'm not sure we can believe a single word coming out of his mouth."

"Well, Judge, it seems that I have just been called a liar by a lawyer who's barely reached puberty."

Avery reached for her gavel and slammed it—something she rarely did. "Stop the name-calling, gentlemen. Look, I'm not going to continue this trial. No way, Mr. Atkins. We're at least going to start with opening statements and the plaintiff's case in chief, and if we need to adjourn at some point to allow a deposition of this witness, we can. If your client wants to file a motion for leave to add Ms. Frankel to its list of witnesses and move to reopen discovery for a deposition of her, I will entertain the motion at that time."

"Judge, I've got Ms. Frankel on the Zoom video right now. I'm making an oral motion that you allow her as a late-identified witness. I think if you hear just five minutes from her, you'll understand what's going on here and why we want to delay this trial and depose her. It will surely be reversible error on appeal if you don't."

At that moment, a middle-aged woman appeared on the video screen. She was dressed in a turtleneck sweater with a vest. That was Avery's first observation. Not the kind of clothing one might typically wear in a tropical location. A woman notices these kinds of things perhaps more than a man does. Also, her pale pink skin appeared to have never seen sunlight. However, it did look like the famous Poás Volcano was behind Ms. Frankel in the background. Actually, on closer inspection, it was obvious that the famous volcano was actually a Zoom background image.

"Well," Avery sighed. "Mr. Atkins, you are being very presumptuous by thinking I am going to entertain this sideshow on the morning of trial."

"But Judge, this is a bench trial. It's not like there's a jury in here that might get confused. You can weigh the credibility of all this and decide whether I might be entitled to call Ms. Frankel as a witness."

Mr. Frankel was squirming like a kid in the school principal's office.

"Judge, please shut this down now!" the Baby-Faced Assassin fired back. "Mr. Atkins's actions continue to create a rancid atmosphere that is now permeating this litigation. He and his clients must be stopped."

Tom whispered to Millicent, "Rancid atmosphere? Whoa! Do you remember just a few months ago when Baby-Face was fighting Hardcore Hank's motion to remand this lawsuit to the state court, and he said that his client was entitled to be in the 'nurturing biosphere' of the bankruptcy court? Atmospheric conditions are changing rapidly around here."

Millicent chuckled quietly.

Judge Lassiter overheard her law clerks and tried not to react. She stared at both lawyers in frustration.

"I think I'd like to ask Ms. Frankel a few questions myself before I decide anything. David, turn on the audio function for me, please."

David, the dutiful courtroom deputy, obliged.

Millicent and Tom looked at each other, unsure where this was heading. The lawyers also seemed a little bewildered.

"Ms. Frankel, this is Judge Lassiter. Can you hear me okay?"

Ms. Frankel fumbled with her muting function. She finally unmuted herself after about thirty seconds of squinting and pushing buttons.

"Yes. I can hear you."

Avery smiled uneasily. "*Pura vida.*"

"Huh?"

"*Pura vida.* Isn't that the proper greeting in Costa Rica?"

"Oh. I guess," Ms. Frankel replied.

"Are you in San Jose, Ms. Frankel?"

"I'm in Costa Rica."

"Yes, but what part? I thought you might be in San Jose?"

"No. I'm out in a very remote area. Near the beach."

Avery hesitated. She knew from a vacation she took once that the Poás Volcano is in the middle of Costa Rica—not on a beach. "Oh. You've got very good internet connectivity, so I just assumed you must be in a city. San Jose, likely."

"Yes. Well, I do have pretty good wireless and internet here."

"Have you seen any sloths?"

Ms. Frankel was silent and looked confused.

Avery tried to make further conversation. "Has the rainy season ended?"

"Oh, thankfully I'm not getting much rain where I am. The sun shines most days. All the time."

Avery hesitated. "Well, except during the rainy season. I've heard that the rainy season in Costa Rica is pretty brutal to endure. Deluges all day long. I was just thinking that this time of year, the rain must still be ongoing for at least a couple of more weeks or so."

Avery looked closely at Ms. Frankel, who was quiet and fidgeting. Avery was starting to feel almost sorry for her—like someone might be taking advantage of her.

"Ms. Frankel, how did you get involved suddenly in this lawsuit. Who reached out to you about this?"

"Should I answer that, Bill? Bill, are you still on the line? Is my personal lawyer Bill on the line? I want to talk to Bill about this."

"Who is Bill, Ms. Frankel?" Avery asked.

Suddenly a new lawyer, who had thus far remained quiescent, appeared on the Zoom video screen. He was a large, white, ruddy-faced bald man with a scowl on his face. He was leaning far back in a black leather recliner. There was a piece of artwork behind him that was rather startling. It looked like a painting of a dead woman in a green business suit, lying face up on a pier. When one quickly glanced at it, it almost looked like it was a window behind the lawyer, with an actual pier with a dead woman on it. The artwork was disturbing by any reasonable person's measure. There was also an end table next to him covered with at least six bottles of a variety of cold medications and lots of tissues. He fumbled with his computer for a few moments, apparently having difficulty turning on the audio function. Before realizing that he had finally activated it, he screamed to someone in the background, "Where's my damn coffee? Has she died or something?"

Avery winced. Maybe "she" was, in fact, the lady in the green business suit and she had, indeed, died.

"I'm Bill Crawford." The lawyer with the scowling face paused for a round of violent coughing. "Your Honor, I of course can't reveal attorney-client privileged or confidential information, but I am at liberty to say that my client, Ms. Frankel, has been out of the country and only recently learned that this lawsuit was still pending and that her ex-husband is claiming that he's owed one hundred million dollars." Another round of coughing ensued for at least thirty seconds before the man regained his composure. "Ms. Frankel believes she has important information about these disputes and has a duty to provide testimony. She reached out to me and then I reached out to Mr. Atkins."

"Ms. Frankel, can you turn your audio and video back on," Avery instructed.

Ms. Frankel complied. As she did, Avery noticed a La Madeleine French Bakery & Café coffee mug in Ms. Frankel's hand. It seemed highly doubtful that La Madeleine had a location in a remote area of Costa Rica.

"I'm sorry, Judge. Did you ask me another question?"

Suddenly, the sound of girls giggling could be heard in the background somewhere near Ms. Frankel. Then a voice could be heard saying, "I'm getting mine to go, Megan. I'm going to the SAE house to study with Scott and his roommate."

Avery looked livid.

"Okay. This sideshow is finished. I don't know if Ms. Frankel has relevant information or not, but I do know she's not in Costa Rica—I'm not sure who is misleading whom on that obvious fact. And the time for discovery has long since passed in this case. You can file a motion, Mr. Atkins, to try to convince me otherwise if you want to, but I caution you to tread lightly, because right now I'm not at all happy. The legal standard to continue the trial at this late date would be a showing of indisputable clarity of necessity. You haven't jumped that hurdle."

Avery looked at the Zoom screen and Ms. Frankel was still there, sipping her La Madeleine coffee.

Avery turned to her courtroom deputy. "David, please disconnect Ms. Frankel from the Zoom. And, also, her lawyer, Mr. Crawford."

Mr. Crawford, with his scowl, creepy artwork, and large collection of cold medicines nearby looked uninterested in and utterly undaunted by anything that had just happened.

David disconnected them.

Millicent whispered to Tom, "Hardcore Hank is definitely entertaining, but his tactics could fill a semester-long law school class on ethics, don't you think? He loves pouring gasoline onto a fire. Wonder if we're ever going to hear anything more about Ms. Frankel again."

Tom replied, "It's like Judge Lassiter sometimes says: 'schadenfreude as a legal strategy.' What could possibly cause a man more misery than having his ex-wife show up as a potential witness for the other side in a business dispute? Maximum pain inflicted—whether it was successful or not. Hank probably thinks this has been a great day for him already."

"Okay, back to business." Avery slid her Tiffany glasses up through her blond bob, rubbed her already tired eyes, and scanned the room. "I'll hear opening statements now. We're starting this trial. Mr. Darby, you may proceed."

The Baby-Faced Assassin tightened his man bun and walked to the lawyer lectern.

Avery was still marveling at the new hairdo. So unexpected from this warrior.

Avery collected herself and focused again on the video screen.

"By the way, Mr. Darby, if this happens to be your PowerPoint up on the screen, can you please do something to make the font readable? Otherwise, I'm going to have to put reading glasses on top of my reading glasses." Avery had already reached for a second pair of glasses.

Millicent whispered to Tom, "More schadenfreude as a legal strategy. The Baby-Faced Assassin is trying to make his much-older adversary miserable by making it nearly impossible for him to read his tiny-font PowerPoint."

Tom winked. "Yup. I think you're right."

4

THE FINANCE BRO

2015, EIGHTEEN MONTHS BEFORE GENEVIEVE MESERO'S DEATH

"Dude, I'm telling you, leverage is one hell of a drug. But when your liquidity dries up—turn out the lights. The party is over. That's where you guys are right now, man. You are worse than just a little cash-challenged. This is where the rubber meets the road. You need to toggle to some different strategies. You're preaching serenity from the edge of the volcano's mouth right now, but your bankers aren't buying any of it."

The Finance Bro. His actual name was Blake Martin. Handsome, polished, smirky, and absolutely full of himself. And listening to the man was utterly exhausting. He was on his third phone call of the evening, trying to pitch corporate restructuring work to a large company that was in financial distress—or "facing some industry headwinds," to use the Finance Bro's cool-guy terminology. Every guest in the posh, dark Dallas restaurant could overhear his loud, cliché-laden macho talk. It was amazing that no restaurant patron had complained yet. The waitstaff seemed hesitant to admonish him, given that he had become a regular diner who was a big spender and passed around ridiculously large tips. His thirty-something, beautiful, brown-eyed, wafer-thin date—hotel heiress Genevieve Mesero—was on her third Sparkling Cosmo of the evening and didn't seem to really care what the Finance Bro was doing as she scrolled through social media on her phone.

"You guys are burning through your cash like you have a hole in your pocket. You haven't had positive EBITDA in months. Your hockey-stick projections that your CFO keeps cranking out are a joke. Nobody is buying his bullshit. He's tilting at windmills, dude. Your banks are breathing down your neck and, any minute now, are going to start exercising the ancient right of self-help. They'll seize everything they can get their greedy little paws on. Or worse, they'll transfer their debt to some bloodthirsty private equity guys. All you can do at this point is start squirreling away your cash and hope that your company can make a soft landing. And I'm telling you, dude, y'all don't have the right CFO to land that plane. God, the guy is untethered to reality. Your board should have canned his ass a long time ago. He's like a lost ball in tall grass. You should have cleared out most of your C-suite, to be honest. Deadwood, most of them. Not a nimble bone in their bodies. They have missed more opportunities to right the ship in the past ten months than I can count. Your industry has been going through a paradigm shift for years now, dude, and it somehow caught them all blindsided. I mean, it's not like what's happened in this space has been a black swan event that no one saw coming."

A waitress came by the table and mouthed something indiscernible, and the Finance Bro shooed her away. The waitress looked at Genevieve with an air of sympathy. Genevieve shrugged.

"Anyway, I'll tell you what you need to do. It's time to pivot. You're at an inflection point. Let me find you some fresh powder—a bridge loan—and we can start marketing the company ASAP. There are lots of potential merger partners out there who would be a great fit and might want to marry their platforms with yours. Create some real synergies with you. It's not a long shot. You all have lots of core competencies that plenty of companies would want to exploit. But let's be real. You just don't have the bandwidth in certain key areas to hit your optimum growth. If you give me some runway, I'll find a stalking horse for you in a month. They'd, of course, want to have a short period of due diligence. But I guarantee we could make it a win-win for everyone. Someone will see you as a real value-added option for them. Hey, wait wait wait, dude. Hang on a second. Hold that thought. I've got another call coming in from Singapore. I've been waiting for this call all day. Different time zones and all. Be back at you in a flash."

The Finance Bro pulled away from his phone. "Hey, babe. You look thirsty. You want another Sparkling Cosmo?"

"Sure, Blake. Why not." The Finance Bro's bewildered date rolled her big brown eyes—such sad eyes—but he didn't seem to notice or didn't care.

The Finance Bro waved his hand, with his well-groomed nails and Wharton class ring flashing, toward a perky, blond waitress in a tight black dress—the one whom he had just waved away two minutes earlier. She dutifully returned with a toothy smile because she knew she'd get a good tip from him. She was new at this restaurant, but she knew his type very well. The type that tipped big to impress, not out of gratitude.

The Finance Bro quickly returned to his Singapore phone call. "Hey, dude. What's shaking? It's T-minus twenty until your deal closes! Everything ready? No? What? What the fuck? Those sons of bitches are trying to move the goalposts on you again? Holy shit! They're a pre-revenue company, for crying out loud. Who do those bastards think they are? Is it time for me to have a come-to-Jesus meeting with their investment banker?"

This was the worst date of Genevieve Mesero's life. Or maybe she had hit the jackpot. She couldn't decide which yet. The Finance Bro was the most obnoxious man with whom she had ever been on a date—no question. And he had no clue how obnoxious he was. Blake Martin was just an investment banker, for crying out loud. But he talked like he was a Navy Seal or some special ops guy who was saving corporate America, one company at a time. He definitely seemed rich as hell. That was at least one thing he had going for him. A house in the Hamptons. Vacation home in Vail. Sports cars. Impromptu trips to places like Lake Como and Positano.

Gigi had been consulting with the Finance Bro for several weeks now—after her bleak trip through personal bankruptcy—about putting together new financing for her family's holding company Belleza Mistica Properties, LLC, which she and her sister had inherited unexpectedly from her father, the legendary Guillermo Mesero, in recent months. Gigi was "over her skis," as the Finance Bro liked to say. Gigi had little preparation for running the company she had inherited. She had earned a BA in Art History from the University of Texas and then backpacked around Europe for a couple of years. She had gone to work for the family's hospitality business after that—begrudgingly—for lack of any other opportunities and no husband prospects on the horizon. She hated the business side of it all and was completely overwhelmed. The only thing Gigi liked about the business was designing and redecorating hotel space when it was time for giving their numerous hotel properties facelifts. Her father had been planning a new resort hotel in the Texas Hill Country (to be named Lacey Oaks; Gigi had chosen that) at the time of his death. Both Gigi and her now co-owner sister Valentina, who was barely more business savvy than Gigi, wanted to complete his dream but were ill-equipped to accomplish it. Then the Finance Bro entered the picture. He heard from a friend of a friend that the Mesero sisters were looking for help. They needed more help than they even realized. Belleza Mistica Properties, LLC, was a multinational, multibillion-dollar company now being run by two relatively young sisters with very little experience.

The Finance Bro seemed like a total idiot to Gigi. His self-esteem seemed absurdly inflated. But he was apparently more complex than she appreciated. She had come to learn that he had a reputation as sort of a bare-knuckle money brute. Apparently, he not only could find capital for his clients, but he frequently got sued (and countersued) at some point before, during, or after the whole fundraising process. This naturally made Gigi worried whether he was the right solution for her complicated business problems. She had heard that he could be like a human bulldozer that tried to obliterate any human atom that questioned him or stood in his way—and he would typically engage in this through lawsuits. Here, there, and everywhere. He had no tolerance. No forgiveness. Only the pervasive desire to conquer. He seemed to live by a code: If you cross me, or I simply don't like what you do, I will make you pay, through either money judgments or litigation costs that you cannot afford. A landscape of lawsuits brought for and against him—usually involving either business partners or clients with whom he had become bitterly divided. He kept his attorneys fat and happy until he turned on those attorneys, as he would inevitably do. Unrelenting, intractable, gut-kicking. That's how a lot of people described him. Nevertheless, Gigi decided to give Finance Bro a try. Her father's legacy depended on it.

It was initially all business with the Finance Bro. He was definitely a top-notch investment banker (despite his obnoxious demeanor), and he seemed to be working hard to find capital for Belleza Mistica. But the Finance Bro had gotten sort of flirty recently (he tended to do that with all women, actually), and Gigi sort of liked it, so she decided to meet him tonight at the newest five-star restaurant in Uptown for drinks, dinner, and "whatever." He'd actually said that, "whatever," when asking Gigi out for the evening. Sure, he was loud and a bit off-putting—and only slightly handsome—but she was so overwhelmed with the corporate world into which she had been thrust that she was willing to entertain the outrageous notion of a romantic relationship with this guy. It might be her way out. Her desperation disgusted her a little. Anyway, the Finance Bro was flying out early the next morning to London, and the restaurant he had suggested for tonight was right down the street from his suite at the Ritz Carlton. Gigi wasn't sure where this was going but for now, she was aimlessly playing along.

His lingo was exasperating, to say the least.

Gigi's head was starting to throb. Why was she doing this? What would her father think of this guy? Would he possibly respect him?

Gigi soon found herself eavesdropping on the Finance Bro's fifth phone call of the evening that he "had to take." It was beginning to seem like every phone call was of this variety.

"Hey, amigo. Let me put a finer point on this. These things rarely work themselves out organically. Hope is not a strategy. Comprende? You're going to have to change your business model. Change your whole mindset. Toggle in a new direction. You're low-hanging fruit right now. Some vulture investor is coming to gobble you up soon! They're circling the wagons. I tell you, there are financial terrorists out there. Before long, queue up the theme song from the *Titanic*. You are going down."

The Finance Bro looked up at Gigi. He whispered, covering up the phone, "Hey, babe. Do you want to order a bottle of wine now? They've got a fantastic selection here. How about a Bordeaux? Didn't you tell me your late mother was French?"

Wow, Gigi thought to herself. *He actually remembered something about me that doesn't involve my company or my money.*

Gigi stood up, wobbly from too many Sparkling Cosmos, grabbing her black Prada purse. She batted her moist brown eyes, blew Finance Bro a kiss, and whispered "later," gracefully exiting the restaurant. She then caught a taxi back to her penthouse at the Mystic Spires Hotel. It was her family's original property in the U.S. Her father had been so happy at its grand reopening. But it now seemed like a sad, withering flower. Gigi felt she was a bit the same.

5

MARVIN BOWERS WAS A SCOUNDREL

1986, THIRTY YEARS BEFORE GENEVIEVE MESERO'S DEATH

"Avery, what are you doing?"

Max walked into the Lassiters' master bedroom after a late evening jog. Avery was propped up with a glossy magazine in her hands and Jake and Finley at her feet. Jake and Finley were the Lassiters' newest pair of Cavalier King Charles spaniels. They were both looking cautiously at Max.

"Honestly, Max. I don't know how you muster the energy to jog at nine at night. Anyway, I'm just reading some folklore about the Mystic Spires Hotel. I found a story in an old *D Magazine* from 1986 about the Marvin Bowers scandal. I don't know if you remember that. It was absolutely crazy."

"Nope. And I can't believe your continuing obsession with that hotel and Gigi. No offense, Avery, but it's almost like you need counseling over it."

"Oh my gosh, Max. I can't believe you said that. You think I am mentally ill because I care?"

"That's not what I meant to imply. It's just that it's starting to seem like you spend a lot of your leisure time reading everything you can about Gigi and her family and the Mystic Spires. I know you. It's your tendency to be the avenging angel. That's what this is."

“What? That’s just wrong. Avenging angels are supposed to be out to punish wrongdoers. To bring wrath to mortals. That’s not who I am, Max.”

“No. Maybe I used the wrong term. I just meant that you so often want to right wrongs and bring justice to situations. You know you are that way, Avery. You can’t just leave that sort of thing at work. It has to be more than your day job. You are twenty-four seven out to stop injustice. That’s what I think all your research is about. You are hoping you will stumble upon something in Gigi’s past or the hotel’s past that will be a new clue to the mystery of her death. I think that the recent fire over there triggered it with you all over again. You obsessed over Gigi’s death for about a year. Then you put it aside. And now it seems to have started up all over again, since the Mystic Spires burned down for good this time.”

Avery sat for a moment in silence. “I wonder if they are going to try to rebuild it?”

“They are not going to rebuild it.”

“Well, I don’t know what to say about your accusation. Let’s just leave this conversation here. I’m going downstairs to make some hot tea. And then I am finishing this article.”

Avery flashed a smirk at Max. He rolled his eyes. The dogs followed Avery downstairs, hoping that a dog treat was in their future.

Avery put on a kettle of water to boil. She got out some Earl Grey tea, then sat down at the kitchen table and resumed her *D Magazine* article. It was all about the infamous Marvin Bowers and his crimes and escapades circa 1986—some of which centered around the Mystic Spires.

Marvin Bowers was a scoundrel. He was a scoundrel by anybody’s standards. He looked like one, with his pastel polyester suits, ostrich-skin boots, salon-tanned face, mustache, and wavy, long brown hair. And he sounded like one, too, with his pretend Southern accent and flamboyant mannerisms. But did he really have an incestuous affair with his aunt? And then conspire with her to kill her rich husband? Damn right, he did. And this was just the beginning.

Marvin Bowers was a "businessman," as people sometimes vaguely say when their jobs—their careers, their professions, their income-producing activities—are a bit shifting or amorphous. He was mostly a real estate investor, or "flipper"—whenever he could find someone to give him money for that. He actually engaged in many commercial endeavors throughout his life—another oblique euphemism, whenever specific examples are hard to articulate or are better left unsaid. Some say Marvin Bowers was nothing but a con man. Indeed, he spent a year behind bars once in California for a check-kiting scheme before he made his way to Texas. Upon arriving in the Lone Star State, Marvin Bowers had difficulty finding any job that he considered suitable, given that he had a recent criminal conviction and rather high income expectations. Marvin Bowers's mother suggested that he call her sister, Aunt Trudy. Why? Because Aunt Trudy had a wealthy multi-business-owning husband whom she had married five years earlier after being widowed. Marvin Bowers decided to do just that.

Before long, Bowers was working for his uncle-by-marriage, who was named Oscar Trueblood. Bowers even moved into Aunt Trudy and Uncle Oscar's fancy North Dallas mansion. And within a year, he was having an incestuous affair with his Aunt Trudy, who was twenty years his senior (perhaps the latter fact was the least weird part of this twisted tale).

Uncle Oscar soon found out about the affair. He was angry, of course. He kicked Marvin Bowers out of his mansion. Oscar was contemplating divorcing Trudy but worried about damage to his reputation if word of the salacious affair was made public. He also had a prenuptial agreement with Trudy in which he had promised she would get half of his wealth if they divorced after at least five years of marriage. Inconveniently, they had just reached that five-year milestone.

Oscar and Trudy separated, but it was awkward. Trudy received a monthly stipend from Oscar, but it was not nearly enough for her many wants and needs. Trudy eventually loaned some of her money to Bowers to buy a nightclub. Bowers's employees reported that Trudy would often come to the business on afternoons. She was overheard complaining about her desire to be free of Oscar and lamenting what a wretched person he had become. He was cutting off her funds and refusing to give her a divorce. Trudy had moved into a luxury suite at the Mystic Spires Hotel—the very one in which Gigi Mesero would be found dead thirty years later.

Soon after that, Oscar Trueblood was found bludgeoned to death by the swimming pool at his North Dallas mansion. Trudy found Oscar's body when she went to the mansion, allegedly to get some clothes. Two months later, both Marvin Bowers and Trudy were indicted for murder.

After a sensational three-week trial, Marvin Bowers and Trudy were acquitted. It was hard to comprehend the acquittal since they had *motive* (Trudy stood to inherit everything if Oscar died—but she would only get half of everything if they divorced) and *opportunity* (Trudy still had keys and access to the mansion and there was no sign of a break-in). Moreover, the direct evidence was substantial: Marvin Bowers's fingerprints were everywhere, and his car, a 1984 red Coupe DeVille, had been seen at the mansion and was later discovered to have traces of Oscar's blood in the trunk. Of course, it was not the first time that guilty folks had gone free, and it would not be the last. Trudy and Marvin Bowers rode off into the proverbial sunset (in the red Coupe DeVille), and Trudy inherited Oscar's entire multimillion dollar estate.

Shockingly, Bowers and Trudy's relationship did not last. Trudy sold the North Dallas mansion and purchased the penthouse at the Mystic Spires Hotel (which she had earlier only temporarily rented). Marvin Bowers lived there at the penthouse with her for a bit. But soon Trudy had a new love interest—yet another man who was twenty years younger than her. The new boyfriend, Cameron, was an aspiring but never-published writer that she met at an Alcoholics Anonymous meeting. That relationship ended when Cameron either fell, jumped, or was pushed to his death from the penthouse. The coroner could not make a determination of which, and no witness saw anything. Trudy was passed out drunk when it happened.

Eventually Trudy died from an overdose of painkillers at the Mystic Spires. Similar to poor Genevieve Mesero, she would be found sprawled out on her bed (a waterbed—it was, after all, the 1980s) in silk pajamas, with music playing and champagne nearby. If that was not a strange enough coincidence, her sister (Marvin Bowers's mother) was the one who found her. In any event, Trudy bequeathed the penthouse to her nephew/former lover

Marvin, with whom she had maintained a cordial relationship. After all, they shared an eternal bond of sorts—Oscar Trueblood's death. By the time of Trudy's pill overdose, Marvin Bowers was worth eight hundred million dollars. He had finally found his true talent (or got lucky) flipping big-ticket commercial real estate. He owned many office buildings in Austin, a yacht named *Mary Lou*, and lots of cars.

Marvin Bowers got a little too risky. When the real estate market took a bad turn, his real estate empire crumbled, and he was on the hook for hundreds of millions of dollars of real estate debt he had guaranteed. He eventually filed personal bankruptcy. And, yes, he claimed the 10,000-plus-square-foot luxurious penthouse at the Mystic Spires he had inherited from Aunt Trudy as his exempt homestead. The strategy worked. His creditors couldn't touch it. As in life, history often repeats itself in the world of business and bankruptcy. Marvin Bowers's legal strategy would be repeated (with success) several years later by a young, financially strapped Genevieve Mesero.

Bowers rebounded from his financial woes, but his health ailments eventually caused him an early death. He died at age fifty-five of a heart attack while aboard his newest yacht, the *Vicky Mae*. He had been sailing around the Bahamas with his newfound love, a twenty-three-year-old stripper from Houston, when he suffered his cardiac event. By the time the coast guard got to the *Vicky Mae* in response to a distress call, Bowers's stripper girlfriend was wearing a full-length blue fox coat with an orange string bikini underneath. She was sobbing uncontrollably. Her name was Vicky Mae. She soon became a media starlet. A picture of her with her orange bikini showing underneath the blue fox coat was plastered in tabloids far and wide.

Marvin Bowers died without a will or children. Vicky Mae would spend the next several years attempting to get what was left of Bowers's estate. The only heirs and heiresses to cause her a fight were Bowers's nephews and nieces, who had supposedly developed a great affection for their uncle in recent years, unbeknownst to anyone who had ever known him.

The sharp whistle from Avery's kettle startled her from her reading. She put down her magazine, picked up the kettle, and poured the steaming water over her tea strainer of Earl Grey. She used a china cup that she had inherited from her mother. She couldn't help but be reminded of all those high teas she, her mother, and her sister enjoyed at the Mystic Spires.

Jake and Finley carefully watched Avery as she took a lemon and sliced it and put some in her tea. She indulged by squeezing in a bit of orange-blossom honey as well.

Avery knew she would lie awake for hours pondering over the Marvin Bowers scandal. What was it about this old hotel?

6

MOTHER TRUCKER— A FIRE AT THE MYSTIC SPIRES

1996, TWENTY YEARS BEFORE GENEVIEVE MESERO'S DEATH

Avery was having lunch at her desk after a morning of continuing shenanigans in her case *Frankel v. Cronus Consulting*, involving Hardcore Hank and the Baby-Faced Assassin. She was picking at her leafy salad, distracted by thoughts of the recent fire at the Mystic Spires Hotel and also pondering the courtroom tactic of bringing one party's ex-wife in as a potential surprise witness in a business dispute—allegedly from a faraway location in Costa Rica. The lawyers were still haggling over this. It was never pleasant whenever angry or divorcing spouses and business disputes became intertwined in court proceedings. Avery's mind drifted back to a nasty situation more than two decades ago when she was a young lawyer—ironically, it had indirectly involved the Mystic Spires and one of its previous fires. *Carter v. Carter*, circa 1996.

Dr. Elizabeth Carter woke up at the leisurely hour of 8 a.m. one chilly Dallas November morning in 1996, walked downstairs, and touched the button on her new Miele whole bean built-in coffee machine. One frothy cappuccino, coming right up. It was her favorite new appliance in an immaculate kitchen full of the finest machines, gadgets, crystal, and pottery that money could buy. It was a Friday. She sat down at her kitchen table with her laptop and turned on a small TV in the breakfast area. She had taken the day off from her busy North Dallas podiatrist practice. Her husband, Dr. Robert Carter—also a podiatrist with a separate practice in a different part of the metroplex—was in Las Vegas for a podiatry convention. Or so he said. Elizabeth planned to go out for a late morning game of tennis at the Northhaven Country Club, get a massage, and then have lunch with some girlfriends from her book club.

As Elizabeth sipped on her cappuccino and flipped through her emails on her laptop, the local TV news station suddenly caught her attention. Breaking away from the national news coverage regarding President Bill Clinton's recent reelection, the local news reporters excitedly announced that there was a four-alarm fire raging at the Mystic Spires Hotel near downtown Dallas. The hotel had, just two years before, been purchased by the wealthy Mesero family and, thereafter, had hosted grand reopening events attended by celebrities and dignitaries. A reporter on the scene, wearing a windbreaker, ball cap, and way too much red lipstick, gave dramatic descriptions of the out-of-control inferno and the rescues underway among the guests—with firefighters chaotically scrambling in the background. A helicopter hovered, and guests stood on their balconies waving in terror and screaming for help. Cameras panned from one balcony to the next, finally focusing on a twelfth-floor balcony where a middle-aged, gray-pajamaed white man with a crooked sandy blond toupee stood with a leather briefcase in his hand, pulling at a helicopter cable that was beginning to hoist him to safety.

"MOTHER TRUCKER!" Dr. Elizabeth Carter screamed at the top of her lungs. Her cats Luna and Stella immediately scattered.

The man being rescued from the balcony at the Mystic Spires was the other Dr. Carter—her dear, philandering husband—who was quite obviously not in Las Vegas. Standing next to him on the balcony was his longtime secretary, Nancy Stefano. Notably, Dr. Robert Carter allowed himself to be rescued before Ms. Stefano. Possible proof that chivalry was, in fact, dead. Of course, it was important for him to save himself. He was known as the "Godfather of Podiatry" among his professional peer group because of important contributions he had made to the field, including winning a significant legal case at the Supreme Court regarding the advertising rights of podiatrists.

The local Dallas and Fort Worth newspapers had front-page stories the next day, blaring headlines such as "Dr. Robert Carter Rescued from Raging Inferno" and "God Rescues Foot God." The picture of him and Nancy Stefano, the latter of whom was waiting in the background for her turn to be rescued behind her lover, was there for all of Dr. Elizabeth Carter's friends, family, and colleagues to see. The matter of *Carter v. Carter* was filed in the Dallas County Family Court the following Monday. It didn't take long for Dr. Elizabeth Carter's best friend and tennis partner, Abigail Smart—one of Dallas's preeminent domestic relations attorneys—to draft the nastiest petition for divorce that one could imagine. There were more skeletons in Dr. Robert Carter's closets than anyone knew—at least according to Dr. Elizabeth Carter. Alcohol-fueled domestic abuse, gambling, affairs with strippers, and abuse of prescription drugs were just a few of his many alleged problems. It was an ugly divorce that resulted in Dr. Elizabeth Carter taking almost everything that her cheating husband had, including a vacation home at Lake of the Ozarks and fifty percent of his lucrative side businesses that manufactured software and supplies geared toward podiatry practices. Dr. Robert Carter filed bankruptcy personally, as well as for his side businesses, soon after the ink was dry on the divorce judgment. That turned out to be a disastrous legal move.

As it turned out, Dr. Robert Carter had a habit of forgetting to disclose (some might say hiding?) assets. When a subpoena was served on Ms. Nancy Stefano, she sang like a bird. She revealed that there was a secret house in Baker's Bay in the Bahamas, another secret house in Lake Tahoe, and gold bars and coins in a secret safe deposit box. It was like a treasure hunt for the bankruptcy trustee, and there was a new jackpot uncovered every week.

Young attorney Avery Lassiter was chagrined and demoralized. She was suddenly drowning in the most unpleasant case that she had endured so far in her budding legal career at the law firm of Madison, Spencer & Collins. She normally did corporate restructuring work at the firm. But because of the business issues involved in Dr. Robert Carter's bankruptcy case, she was drafted to play a role. Her senior partner at the firm, Ward Scott, was working on the case with her.

"What are you doing, Avery? It's late."

Ward had just wandered down the hall to Avery's office. It was cluttered with boxes, stacks of paper, and numerous empty Starbucks containers. Ward looked like he was ready to head out for the evening, but Avery was nowhere close.

"Well, I'm working—yet again—on an amended set of asset schedules for the Carter case. Trying to keep the client out of jail for failure to disclose assets. He keeps remembering more stuff that he or his companies own. Today, he asked whether he has to disclose his collection of feet."

"Feet? I'm afraid to hear this, I think."

"Yes, feet, Ward. I guess it should come as no surprise to anybody that a podiatrist has a foot fetish. He has a collection of over two hundred fifty feet that takes up a whole room beside his reception area in one of his suburban offices, about which I only recently learned. The suburban office is in—wait for it, wait for it—*Foothills* Meadows."

Ward winced. "You're not joking, are you, Avery."

"Nope. I wish I was."

"Well, Avery, before you have a nervous breakdown thinking our client is going to go to jail over this, step back and reflect. The foot collection just sounds like office supplies. I'm sure you already have disclosed that Dr. Carter and his company own lots and lots of office supplies, right? I don't think you have to worry that someone would think he's failed to disclose valuable assets if he doesn't specifically mention that some of the supplies happen to be models of feet. I mean, how valuable can a bunch of fake feet be anyway?"

"Uh, these aren't just any fake feet, Ward. It's not like they are made of plastic or papier-mâché or resemble something you might see in a college anatomy class. There are marble feet, porcelain feet, gold-plated feet, sterling silver feet, ivory feet, jade feet. Feet that are proportional to human size and some that are huge."

"Like how huge?"

"Uh, one's about sixty inches across."

"Is that the gold one?"

"No, the ivory one. It was made from a Tanzanian elephant tusk, supposedly."

"Okay. This is weird. No wonder you seem like you're in a foul mood. Better ways to use your legal mind, I suppose, than preparing an inventory of feet."

"Well, I don't mean to be grumpy. It pays the bills, right?"

"Hopefully. We actually haven't gotten our fees paid on this case yet."

"Ugh. Well, I need to follow up on that, I guess. I tell you, Wade, I've learned from this case to not even think about ever getting a divorce. Stick with your spouse no matter what."

"Even if he humiliates you by being caught by news reporters in a fiery inferno with his paramour on a hotel balcony?"

"Well, yes, I suppose there are limits. But I'm just saying I can't believe what divorce does to people. And when you mix divorce and bankruptcy, I'd feel like I needed to wear a bulletproof vest every day, just in case I'm caught in their crossfire."

"I don't know if you're joking or serious, but these things do get ugly, for sure."

"Are you about to recite that old saying about a woman scorned?"

"No. I was actually thinking of an old case involving a man scorned. At least that's what some people thought. Do you remember when you were a summer clerk during law school, and we were working on a financial restructuring for two brothers—the Crockett brothers?"

"I think vaguely. I'm thinking it was an oil field tools company?"

"That's it, Avery. Good memory. Crockett Industries. It was owned by brothers Morris and Clinton Crockett. Founded by their late father 'Ace' Crockett. A Fort Worth oil tycoon."

"Let me guess. Descendants of Davy Crockett?"

"I doubt it since he famously died in the Alamo without any known children. Anyway, several years before the company and the Crockett brothers got into financial trouble, there had been a scandalous divorce involving Clinton and his flashy wife Eva. Clinton went on trial for murder in Fort Worth for supposedly killing Eva's younger boyfriend. Clinton was acquitted but later went on trial for attempted murder of the divorce judge and others."

"Good grief! How did I not know this or remember it? I just remember the oil field tools company. Tell me everything. I need a respite from inventorying Dr. Carter's enormous foot collection."

"I can't believe I'm recounting this story all of these years later at eight at night when I could be watching Monday Night Football."

"Please, you've got me fascinated. Tell me all you can remember."

"Well, let's see. Clinton looked very straitlaced, and he was supposedly very smart and hardworking, but after his very controlling father died, he married Eva. They had begun an affair when they were both still married to other spouses. It was his second marriage and her third or fourth. Eva was over-the-top flashy. Long, platinum blond hair, big eyelashes, tight clothes and plunging necklines, and lots of diamonds."

"Go on. This is fascinating. Sounds like a terrible B movie."

"Well, Clinton and Eva began spending his fortune like crazy. His father had always lived modestly, despite his vast wealth from being a wildcatter, and encouraged that in his sons. But Clinton built a fourteen-million-dollar mansion on a hill overlooking Fort Worth that he and Eva named Cresta de Toro. He filled it with expensive art and furnishings from all over the world. They allegedly had wild, expensive parties there. About six years or so into the marriage, Eva filed for divorce, claiming Clinton had a dark side and had abused her. She soon began dating a former NFL linebacker. Anyway, the divorce got ugly, and Eva was awarded, at least temporarily, the mansion and a nice monthly support payment. One night, Eva came back to Cresta de Toro after a late night with her new boyfriend; they went in the house, and a man in black, wearing a woman's black wig, shot Eva and the boyfriend. The boyfriend was killed. Eva made it outside, running and bleeding, and some friends driving up intervened and one of those friends was shot and ultimately paralyzed for life. One dead and two others seriously wounded."

"This is terrible. Was it definitely Clinton who did it?"

"Well, according to a jury of his peers, there was reasonable doubt, and he was acquitted. He hired a brilliant defense attorney, and he did a brilliant job painting Eva as a gold digger and low-life who hung around with a bad crowd of druggies and suggested one of those bad characters did it."

"What about the divorce judge? You said Clinton was accused of trying to kill him as well?"

"Yeah, he was indicted for trying to put a hit out on him and certain others—I've forgotten all the details—but he got an acquittal on that as well. Once again, his defense attorney made it look like it was a setup and that Eva had convinced the FBI to improperly engage in a sting operation to entrap him."

"Well, that story may just be worse than *Carter v. Carter*. If nothing else, it has reinforced my intention to avoid divorce like the plague."

"Do you have any pictures of the feet, Avery? I have got to see some of those—at least the sixty-inch one made of an elephant tusk."

"Oh, you better believe I've got pictures. Brace yourself for an ocular shock. They are quite a vision to behold."

As Avery reached for a file of pictures on her desk, she paused and asked Ward, "So, I wonder what the status is of the investigation of the fire at the Mystic Spires that started this whole *Carter v. Carter* debacle? Have you heard anything, Ward?"

"Nope. Probably just electrical problems or somebody smoking in bed. I haven't heard of any suspicions of it being anything other than an accidental fire. You know how old hotels are."

Tom knocked on Avery's door, startling her from her daydreaming. It was as though she had been transported back in time. Her law-practice days seemed like a lifetime ago. She was still dealing with failure—did that sound too negative? That's what she did. She dealt with failure. People's failures. Companies' failures. Only as a judge, it was lonelier than it was as a lawyer.

"Judge, is everything okay? It's time to go back into court. You said we would resume at one-thirty p.m. I made a fresh pot of coffee."

"Thanks, Tom. Yes, I'm coming. Let me grab my robe."

7

THE LIONESS AND GUILLERMO MESERO

"The Lioness" was the nickname that Guillermo Mesero, Genevieve and Valentina's late father, had given to their late mother Vivienne.

Vivienne the Lioness was a strong, athletic, honey-blond beauty who was reared the first part of her life at an English countryside estate just outside of Derbyshire's market town of Ashbourne. She was kind and witty and "as genuine as a sunrise," as Guillermo often used to say. She had a spirit of adventure that was almost exhausting.

The Lioness's father was English—Seymour Crane, the wealthy owner of a U.K. shipping company, a cricket player, and an all-around philanderer. He was eventually elected to the English House of Commons where he served two decades before dying of a heart attack in bed with a stripper named Roxie Love. The Lioness's mother, Collette Hodenq, had been a French fashion model (ski fashions and beachwear) and eventually divorced the Lioness's father after one too many of his indiscretions. Collette moved with her small daughter back to her hometown of Chamonix, France, when Vivienne was age ten.

Guillermo met Vivienne when she was just twenty-three years old at the Kitzbuhel ski resort in Austria, where she was convalescing after being injured while training as a hopeful for the Innsbruck Winter Olympics. After that chance meeting, the couple had a long, tumultuous on-again, off-again courtship. Guillermo adored the Lioness and found her fascinating, but he had a passion for and dated other beautiful women. The Lioness tolerated it. She had, after all, grown up with a philandering father, so perhaps she thought all men were this way.

After several years of rendezvousing in romantic spots like Monte Carlo and San Sebastián, Guillermo eventually moved the Lioness (without proposing) to Dallas to be with him. Guillermo was the kind of man who could lure a woman away like that. He was tall and handsome and had a velvety romantic voice. He was an erudite gentleman, and she was a cosmopolitan woman. After moving to Texas, she rambled around his Turtle Creek mansion while he traveled building his hotel empire. The Lioness grew to love Texas, as strange a land as she found it to be. She soon became well known in Dallas high society for her stunning golden tresses and bold and stylish ways. She lived a life full of fun when Guillermo was not around, riding horses and playing polo, which was another passion of hers besides skiing. She took a group of lady friends from the Dallas Junior League to Paris Fashion Week every fall and Wimbledon every summer. The Dallas ladies talked about Vivienne's unconventional ways behind her back, but they were happy to partake of her invitations when they were especially luxurious and gratis. The Lioness also had a few boyfriends on the side from time to time. One rumor was that she had dated musician Don Henley of the Eagles. It may or may not have been true. There was a similar rumor that she dated the singer George Michael—but of course he was gay, so they were only friends.

Guillermo and the Lioness finally got married after a nine-year courtship and soon after that had Gigi and Valentina. The Lioness remained an intrepid traveler to exotic places even after the girls were born and, sadly, she died one spring morning in a plane crash over Martha's Vineyard when Gigi and Valentina were ages four and two.

Guillermo never got over the loss of his beautiful Lioness—his French English rose, fearless and free. He regretted having treated her badly in the early years of their relationship. He put a large oil painting of the Lioness, regally sitting next to her two young daughters, all dressed in blue satin, in the lobby of every one of his hotel properties. For the rest of his days, he doted on Gigi and Valentina. He treated them like princesses. He was determined to leave them a legacy. Fabulous wealth. A corporate dynasty. He would never let any man hurt them.

Guillermo was born in Mexico City. His parents had immigrated there from Lebanon in the early 1900s. After attending college in the U.S., he returned to Mexico City, where he met a young Carlos Slim who, like Guillermo, had Lebanese Mexican heritage. After working together as stock traders, Slim hired Guillermo to run his real estate company he eventually established. From there, Guillermo got involved in Slim's hospitality businesses and finally struck out on his own and relocated to Texas. Guillermo had been fascinated with Texas since reading about the American hotel titan Conrad Hilton, who launched his own hotel empire with his very first hotel in Cisco, Texas. Hilton was quoted as saying, "There's a vastness here and I believe that the people who are born here breathe that vastness into their soul. They dream big dreams and think big thoughts, because there is nothing to hem them in." That resonated with Guillermo. He was that same type of dreamer himself. And so was the Lioness. They loved the Texas mystique. It was enormous and yet had a tight cohesiveness.

Guillermo had already started building his own small luxury hotel empire when, at age thirty-two, he met the Lioness that fateful day in Austria.

8

THERE'S SOMETHING ABOUT A COWBOY

FEBRUARY 2016, TEN MONTHS BEFORE GENEVIEVE MESERO'S DEATH

"I think I have figured out what I'm going to do next."

Genevieve Mesero looked wide-eyed at her host and hostess, Tanner and Maddie Swenson. Tanner had been training Gigi with horse grooming and competitive riding recently. Gigi's late mother had been a skilled rider and a polo aficionado back in her day—which had something to do with Gigi taking up this hobby. Gigi was sitting with the Swensons on their back deck at their ranch near Granbury, Texas, having drinks after a big home-cooked meal prepared by Maddie.

"Well, are you going to tell us, Gigi?" asked Maddie.

"I think I'm going to buy a property near Lexington, Kentucky, and develop a boutique hotel there and also raise horses. I've got two possible names picked out for it. One is the Steeplechase Chateaux & Derby Distillery. And yes, I said distillery. I'd make my own brand of bourbon there. My other idea is the Bluegrass Boutique. Or maybe I should just go with the Derby Inn—that would be a dual reference to the Kentucky Derby and also my mom who spent the first few years of her life growing up in the Derbyshire area of England, outside of Ashbourne."

"Gigi, I think all of your time out here training with the horses has made you loopy," said Tanner. "Either that or too many cocktails tonight." Tanner winked at her and poured her another shot of Four Roses Bourbon. Maddie noticed the flirtatious wink and didn't like it.

Tanner had been training Gigi in grooming and riding for about a year now. She was becoming quite a good rider. She had even started entering competitions under Tanner's tutelage. It made Gigi happy like nothing else in recent years. She had sweet memories of her father taking her and her sister to see the famous Lipizzan horses of the Spanish Riding School when they were small children. It was something he said her mother would have done with them had she lived long enough. Gigi also very much enjoyed spending time with Tanner. He was a very handsome and strong man. And he was so genuine, unlike most of the men she knew in Dallas. She joked that he looked like the Marlboro Man. Only a healthier, blond version that didn't smoke. He was not rich, but he didn't care. He had all he needed in life, living on the land and raising horses. She liked it that he didn't care a thing about money and material things.

"Why are you saying I'm loopy, Tanner? It's a great idea. It would give me a chance to be in the horse capital of the world. Or at least the horse capital of the U.S. It's beautiful country, so green and lush, with all those horse farms with rolling hills and white wooden fences. I have it all pictured. It would be a limestone mansion with lots of spires and steeples and weather vanes. There's a place called Versailles on the Bluegrass Parkway near Lexington that gave me the idea. But I know we could put together something much grander."

"We? Who do you mean by we?" Maddie chimed in.

"Well, all of us. You two could be my collaborators on this project. My sister Valentina thinks I'm crazy. My investment banker thinks I'm crazy. They are not supporting me at all on my vision. But I'm going to make it happen, with or without their support. Horses are my true love. I mean it. I love my time out here on this ranch, training with the horses, more than any other thing in my life. So, I'm going to combine my passion with my business."

"Have you even finished the Lacey Oaks Lodge down in the Hill Country yet?" Tanner asked. "It seems like that's been all-consuming, trying to finish that property to honor your father. I thought it was still a bit away from opening day."

"It is. But I have moved on mentally. I've let Valentina take over the reins on that one. I can't stand dealing with my investment banker we've got working on that one with us. He ended up being a mistake, and I'm letting her finish it up. I'm ready to move on."

"Well." Tanner took a long pause. "Maybe you should start slow. Buy some property out here in Granbury and stay out in the country on the weekends. I told you there's a farmhouse on about a hundred acres just a couple of miles from here for sale. You should buy it. Build you some horse stables on it. Buy you a bunch of horses. I could take care of your horses on the weekdays when you're in Dallas, or you could keep your horses here with mine."

Gigi smiled big at Tanner. "I suppose you're right. It would be such great therapy to be out here every weekend. And have a bunch of horses of my own instead of just treating yours as my own. Hell, maybe I'll do both. Buy a weekend property out here and a property to develop in Kentucky. I just really like the idea of being up there and maybe even investing in a thoroughbred ranch. And going to the derby every year. Hosting massive derby parties."

Tanner grinned again. "You know what you need? I think you need to go on a midnight ride. Why don't you go change clothes, put on some of those fancy boots of yours, and I'll get the horses saddled up?"

Gigi laughed. "I'm too drunk. I'd fall off the horse, I'm afraid."

Maddie started picking up glasses and bottles. "You're both too drunk. We're all too drunk."

"I'm afraid my wife is probably right. Maybe we ought to plan on a morning ride instead. At seven a.m.?"

"Oh, maybe we should make it eight a.m. instead. I sleep so well out here in that beautiful guest house that I never want to get out of bed."

"Okay. We will make it eight then. You have everything you need out there in the guest house?"

"Absolutely. Maddie is the hostess with the mostest. In fact, Maddie, why don't you let me help you clean up in the kitchen before I turn in."

"No, please. You go ahead and get some rest."

"No. I insist."

Gigi and Maddie headed into the kitchen. Tanner headed upstairs to bed, pulling off his shirt as he stepped up the stairs. Gigi pretended not to notice, but she did. She noticed his tattoo on his right shoulder blade of the Swenson Ranch logo.

Gigi and Maddie tackled the kitchen mess in silence for a few minutes. Then Maddie turned on some Van Morrison. Gigi wandered over to the credenza behind the breakfast table and looked at some of the Swenson family pictures.

"You know, Maddie, you're so lucky. Living out here in the country. Having a man like Tanner. There's just something about a cowboy, don't you think?"

Maddie looked at Gigi strangely. "What do you know about cowboys, Gigi?"

"Oh. I'm sorry. That sounded . . . well, I'm not sure how it sounded. I am just so sick of the phoniness of my life in Dallas. The country club set. The men that my sister and friends insist on setting me up with. They are all so plastic. So arrogant. So shallow. So boring. Everything about them is a work of pure contrivance. What I really need is a man like Tanner. I wish he had a single twin."

Maddie did not react and washed their glasses in silence.

"Anyway, I just appreciate so much the time he is taking teaching me to ride. He says I'll be ready to compete—really compete in some of the big shows—by spring. And I do appreciate your hospitality letting me stay out here so often. I'm in no shape to drive after a night of drinking like this."

"You're always welcome here, Gigi."

Gigi looked again at the Swenson family pictures.

"Are you looking to see if Tanner has a brother? I can save you the time. He doesn't. Only a sister in Wyoming. Just one sister."

Gigi giggled. "Oh, I'm just admiring what a close-knit family you all seem to have. All these family gatherings over the years. I have a sister, too. But we sort of go our own separate ways for most holidays. I mean, I'm close to her. We love each other. But she has this deadbeat husband I can't stand, Cort. Cort has sort of fractured our relationship in some way. Cort hates me and I hate him. I think he wants to run me out of the business and just have him and Valentina run it."

"Well, if that's the case, maybe you need to focus on preserving what's yours—the dynasty that your father worked so hard to build—and not pursue horses and developments in Kentucky."

Gigi was silent. She kept picking up family pictures. "Maddie, I'm kind of wondering why you and Tanner never had kids. You seem like you would make a great mother and he a great father."

Maddie stared at Gigi with stiff body language that signaled Gigi had gone too far with that question. Gigi realized Maddie was uncomfortable.

"Well, it looks like we have everything cleaned up pretty well here. I guess I'll head out to the guest house and call it a night. I doubt I'm going to need my usual swig of NyQuil to get to sleep tonight."

"What's that?"

"Oh. I have terrible trouble sleeping most nights. I usually have to take an ounce or two of NyQuil to dose off. But I won't have to tonight after all the cocktails and bourbon."

Maddie laughed. "Oh. Better not."

"Good night, Maddie. Thank you for everything. You and Tanner are such a joy to be around."

"Good night, Gigi. And I've got some NyQuil right here in the cabinet above the sink if you decide you need some."

9

SISTERS IN VALENCIA, SPAIN

MARCH 2016, NINE MONTHS BEFORE GENEVIEVE MESERO'S DEATH

"I'm thinking I want to go to Spain for spring break. Valencia, Spain. Down the coast a bit from Barcelona. Would you maybe want to go with me? We can go to the Fallas festival!"

Avery was talking to her sister on FaceTime on a lazy Sunday afternoon while sitting on her back porch with her spaniels, Jake and Finley. The dogs did not like to be ignored when Avery talked on the phone. They occasionally jumped on the lawn furniture and nuzzled next to Avery for attention.

Avery had been begging her sister Suzanne to take a trip with her for ages. Suzanne's life always seemed too busy to get away.

"I don't know. You mean just the two of us?"

"Why not? Or we could take our daughters along to be our chaperones if you think we should?"

Suzanne looked shocked. "Why would we need chaperones, Avery?"

"Oh, you know I'm just being silly. But please think about it. Pretty please, Suzanne?"

Suzanne was multitasking from room to room in her house at a pace that was dizzying. Avery wondered how much she was really focusing on her travel suggestion.

"Have you gone to Valencia before, Avery? I can't remember. You seem to have been everywhere on the planet at least once. I lose track of all your adventures."

"Yeah, I've been there twice."

"So why do you want to go again? Why not go somewhere new? And you know me. I'm really more of a Cape Cod kind of girl. Valencia seems a little too exotic for my tastes. And I just hate long flights."

"Valencia is probably my favorite place in Spain. I could never get tired of it. It's on the Mediterranean. Great climate. Great food. Paella and sangria—the city claims to have invented paella. And the city is a combination of medieval cobblestone streets and Gothic architecture on one side, and a modern, sleek city on the other. There's a golden, clean beach with a really cool aquarium next to it. Bullfighting is still legal at the Plaza de Toros. And, of course, they have the Fallas festival."

"Bullfighting," Suzanne shuddered. "There is no way I'm ever going to a bullfight with you. Never. I cannot believe you like bullfighting. It sounds absolutely barbaric."

"It's not as horrific as you think, Suzanne."

"That's not exactly a ringing endorsement. There's all that blood."

"Okay. I won't force the issue on that! Maybe I'll do that one afternoon by myself and you can go to a spa or something."

A month later, Avery and Suzanne were on holiday in Valencia with their daughter-chaperones, Julia and Kat.

The month prior, Avery had caught Suzanne up on the ins and outs of the Fallas festival, that annual celebration of Saint Joseph in Valencia (otherwise a celebration of spring for the non-Catholics) that happens every March. Similar in atmosphere to New Orleans's Mardi Gras, Venice's and Rio de Janeiro's Carnivale, or Mexico's Día de los Muertos, it featured music, food stands, and street parties—only a little more family-oriented. Instead of floats, the celebrations have hundreds of giant colorful cardboard and papier-mâché monuments (*ninots*, which means dolls or puppets in Valencian) that are scattered about the city and are filled with firecrackers and burned in bonfires at the end of the multiweek festival. "Fallas" is derived from a Latin word that means torch. There are firecrackers all day, every day—especially a magnificent display at 2 p.m. near city hall known as "Mascletà." It is noisy all day and all night. Similar to New Orleans during Mardi Gras, each neighborhood of the city has an organized group of people who work all year long holding fundraising parties and dinners to pay for the construction of their *ninot* monuments, which are often more than fifty feet high. They are vibrant, dramatic, and beautiful. People vote on the best monument, and the winning monument each year is preserved in a museum, rather than burned. Many of the monuments feature political or satirical themes or celebrities. On the final night of Fallas, around midnight, when the monuments are burned, it is known as Noche de la Cremà ("the burning"), and it is the climax of the whole event.

"This place is amazing. You didn't oversell it, Avery. I'm glad we came." Suzanne reached for a pitcher of white sangria made with cava that was almost empty.

The two of them, plus Julia and Kat (who were mostly glued to their phones), were in a quaint tapas bar and café called Restaurante Lienzo, overlooking the historic Serranos Towers in the Carme area of the city.

"Girls, did you save room for chocolate and churros? That's next. Kat, are you buying?"

Kat looked up from her phone at her Aunt Avery, looking a little bored. "I will always say yes to anything chocolate."

Avery continued. "I figure we can stop and get some chocolate and churros on the way down to the Silk Exchange, which is several blocks from here. They call it La Lonja. After that we can go down to this spectacular thirteenth-century Gothic-style church called the Cathedral of Valencia that has possession of what they claim is the Holy Grail. It's on display in a special chapel."

"What's the Holy Grail, Mom?" Julia asked her mother.

"Good God. You don't know? I guess I have completely failed as a mother. It's the Holy Chalice that Jesus drank out of at the Last Supper."

Julia's face showed its usual ornery skepticism. "I bet they are totally making that up, Mom. It sounds like a tourist trap for sure."

"The wisdom of a seventeen-year-old. You're going to be struck by lightning for saying that, Julia."

Julia rolled her eyes at her mother. Kat giggled.

Suzanne scanned the room as she took her last couple of sips of sangria. "Oh my God, Avery. Look over to your right at the table in the corner. I mean, be cool and nonchalant about it. But you've got to look. There are two women—have to be in their late thirties—all decked out like they're about to walk the runway. Except that they have the Valencia traditional blue plaid scarves around their necks. 'When in Rome,' I guess? Or an effort to blend? Anyway, the scarves are a real mismatch for their Carolina Herrera clothing and those stylish Miron Crosby boots. But I digress. Anyway, I think it's Gigi and Valentina Mesero. The hotel heiresses from Dallas."

Kat and Julia whipped around, not being at all subtle.

"Girls!" Suzanne snapped. "You're embarrassing us. I said to be nonchalant about it!"

"You only told my mom to be nonchalant about it," Julia quipped.

Avery dropped her napkin on the floor and then casually glanced over to her right as she picked it up.

Julia and Kat giggled at her. "Smooth move, Mom. That wasn't obvious at all."

Avery ignored their sarcasm. "Suzanne, I think you are right. It's them. Gigi had a case in my court a little while back. I'd recognize her anywhere. Wow. Imagine that. Two sisters vacationing in Valencia just like us. Only they are really rich and are probably staying in much nicer digs than us. I wonder if they own a hotel over here. Maybe there's a Mystic Spires Valencia that I don't know about. Wonder how you say Mystic Spires in Spanish."

"Nope, they don't have one," Julia said.

"Huh?"

"There's not a Mystic Spires Hotel in Valencia. I just Googled their website." Julia looked up from her phone with satisfaction. "See?"

Avery craned her head to look over at Julia's phone.

"Oh, and Mystic Spires in Spanish is Agujas Místicas."

"Oh you're such a clever girl, Julia. I'm so glad I paid for the international plan for your smartphone. It's coming in very handy right now, for sure. Anyway, I guess the Mesero sisters are just vacationing like us ordinary folks."

"But I sort of would have pictured them to be more the type to vacation in Barcelona or Marbella," Suzanne stated.

"Well, maybe they are just in Valencia for a day trip to enjoy a few hours of Fallas," Avery replied. "You can get here in a couple of hours by train from either Barcelona or Marbella."

"Train? *Train?* You think those women travel by train like mere mortals?" Suzanne said before sipping her sangria.

"You'd be surprised. 'When in Europe,' ya know? And Gigi was in a personal bankruptcy case not too long ago. Maybe she has had to adjust her living standards."

"Nope. I bet they have a hundred-foot yacht waiting for them out in the bay, all set to take them over to Mallorca."

"Only a hundred-foot yacht? I'm not sure that's very big for a yacht, Suzanne. Julia, why don't you Google that."

About that time, Avery and Suzanne were distracted as two men joined the Mesero sisters. One man was a well-dressed Latino with wavy, thick dark hair and a mustache, and the other one looked like a boyish, well-built, blond Texas cowboy. Both were tall and very handsome. Each had a bouquet of flowers for the women.

"Well, well, well. The plot thickens." Suzanne put down her drink with a clang. "Boyfriends? They are traveling in Spain with boyfriends? This is scandalous! I read that Gigi supposedly dates some skinny, pale investment banker who isn't very attractive but has more money than God. And Valentina is supposedly estranged from her husband Cort—who doesn't seem like a very impressive guy, by the way. He is apparently some sort of a moocher who has wormed his way into their hotel business. But she's definitely still married. I've seen pictures of him with Valentina recently in the *Dallas Observer*, and he doesn't look anything like either one of those two men."

"Suzanne, it could just be a business meeting," Avery chimed in. "Maybe those men are people in the hotel industry, and they're discussing a business deal with the Meseros. Or they could be relatives. Or casual friends."

At that moment, the Mesero sisters shrieked with laughter, and Gigi leaned over and kissed the Texan-y cowboy.

"Uh, Mom, get real. I would never kiss a relative or a friend like Gigi just kissed that cowboy-looking man." Julia was now contributing to the conversation.

"You're right," Avery and Suzanne said in unison.

Avery, Suzanne, and their girls all stared at the Mesero sisters' table with more than a passing interest. All efforts at nonchalance had been abandoned. The Mesero sisters were drinking what appeared to be vodka tonics like it was water. The laughter and occasional kisses with their male friends continued.

Avery suddenly jolted from her stare. "Okay. This is ridiculous. I can't believe our behavior. We need to pay our check and get out of here. We've got better things to do than eavesdrop on these people. It's rude and weird. I'm embarrassed. Curious, but embarrassed. Besides, we need to get out of this Plaça de l'Ajuntament area before two p.m. when the pyrotechnics start. If we don't make an exit in the next ten minutes or so, we'll be trapped in a crush of people like a bunch of sardines for at least an hour." With that, Avery waved down the waiter and they were soon gone, taking one last peek at the Mesero sisters' table before leaving.

Hours later, Avery and Suzanne were resting on a stone bench at a plaza outside of a Gothic church called Santa Catalina. They had just climbed seven stories up its spiral staircase to its spectacular baroque bell tower to view the city. They were now enjoying some gelato and a live band while the girls wandered around taking selfies by some beautiful fountains, posing with colorful characters in medieval costumes.

"Is this safe, you think, Avery? I mean, letting the girls roam around out there by those fountains with those characters? Does this city have any problems with human sex traffickers that maybe secretly pose as happy characters during Fallas?"

"Oh my God, Suzanne. You may be the one and only human being in the world that is more paranoid than me."

The girls suddenly approached their mothers. "Mom, will you give me a few euros to go over to that pharmacy and get some Band-Aids? I've got a bad blister." Julia pointed to her ankle.

"Ouch. Sure, sweetie. The pharmacy is the store that has a green cross sign out front. And watch out for human sex traffickers." Avery handed Julia some euros.

Julia looked annoyed. "Mom! I know what the green cross symbol means! Do you think I'm a child? How'd you think I knew that there was a pharmacy over there to begin with?"

"Excuse me, Julia. I forgot that you are almost seventeen years old and very worldly. What was I thinking!"

Kat jumped up. "I'll go with you, Julia."

The two of them headed off to the pharmacy.

Avery and Suzanne lingered watching the crowds and festivities, savoring their last bites of gelato.

A few moments later the girls returned.

"Did you find Band-Aids, sweetie?"

"Yep. And guess who I saw inside the pharmacy."

"I don't know. Tell me, Julia."

"The Mesero sisters. And their hot boyfriends."

"Oh great. They probably think that we're stalking them now."

"Gigi was buying NyQuil," Kat said.

"Good lord. Y'all are so nosey. Let a woman buy NyQuil in peace!"

Suzanne chimed in. "Wonder why Gigi would be buying NyQuil? She sure didn't seem like she had a cold at lunch. She looked as bubbly and perky as a woman can be. She doesn't have a cold, I tell you."

"Maybe the flowers from her boyfriend caused her allergies to suddenly flare up or something," Julia theorized.

"Nope," Kat replied. "I heard her telling the pharmacy manager that she needed NyQuil to help her sleep. She told him that she always takes NyQuil at nighttime in the U.S., and she was asking if it had the same amount of alcohol content as the kind of NyQuil that's sold in the U.S. The pharmacist seemed totally confused, like he couldn't really understand what she was asking him. And he kept trying to offer her something else as a sleep aid."

"Yeah," Julia confirmed. "She kept saying she didn't want to take anything that might have too much codeine or some other drug that might be addictive."

"Sounds like she might be addicted to NyQuil, if you ask me," Suzanne replied. "And I don't think she should be taking NyQuil after all of those vodka tonics she was having at lunch. She could go into liver failure or something."

"Oh, good God. I cannot believe we are having this conversation. We're in one of the most beautiful cities in the world and we are debating why Gigi Mesero was buying NyQuil, for crying out loud. And anyway, could you blame Gigi for needing a little help getting to sleep here? There are fireworks and music all day and all night!" Avery noticed that Suzanne and Julia were not paying much attention to her, only staring back at the pharmacy for another glimpse at hotel royalty.

Avery sighed and shook her head.

"Okay. Julia, put on your Band-Aid and let's go look at more *ninots*. Hopefully we won't get kidnapped by any human traffickers posing as beautiful medieval characters."

10

A CRIMINAL NAMED WORM

JUNE 2017, SIX MONTHS AFTER GIGI MESERO'S MURDER

"Whatcha doing, sweetie pie?"

Max swiveled around from his computer in the family room. "I'm looking for a criminal named Worm."

"Worm?"

"Yes, Avery. Worm."

"Wonder why he goes by the nickname Worm?"

"Why do you assume it's a nickname and not the person's legal name given at birth?"

"What? Please tell me Worm is not his legal name."

"It's not. But, actually, would you believe there are thirty convicted criminals in the Dallas Police Department computer database who go by the nickname Worm?"

"No way!"

"Way."

"What on earth does a man named Worm look like? Is he tall and skinny with beady eyes? Kind of slinky like an invertebrate?"

"Why do you assume it's a he? I never said Worm was a he."

"Well, I guess Worm sounds like it would be a he. I mean, Worm is a he, right? I would think all thirty Worms in your police database are he's, right?"

"Avery, does it really matter?"

"I don't know. I guess not. I'm mainly just baffled that thirty alleged criminals in Dallas would all go by the nickname Worm, regardless of their gender. What did the current Worm that you're looking for allegedly do?"

"Nice that you're being all judgy and using the word 'allegedly.' There's no 'allegedly' on this one, trust me. The current Worm is crawling through doggie doors of large homes in North Dallas while the owners are away and stealing jewelry and small electronics. He throws his stolen bounty into a duffle bag, makes his getaway on a motor scooter, and pawns it. We've got lots of Ring doorbell camera footage. You can see his Worm tattoo on his left arm. We have also gotten pawn shop camera footage of the tattoo. Anyway, Worm's making a very good living off of it. Very good."

"Oh, now I get it. He's called Worm because he's obviously skinny and wormy enough to worm his way through a doggie door."

"Well, doing meth will make a person pretty skinny like that. But not sure that's why he's called Worm. Another one of the criminal Worms that I arrested weighed two hundred fifty pounds. Remember that guy who was high on PCP who broke into a ninety-year-old man's house wearing a vest made out of porn magazines and was swinging around kitchen knives at the old man's caretaker?"

"Yeah, and I remember he was also swinging around things at you when you rushed into the house to arrest him. How could I forget? That was the time you lost your wedding ring."

"Well, yes. And I almost lost my life, I suppose. But nice that you would focus only on the lost wedding ring and not my injuries."

"Ah, 'twas only a flesh wound. Well, several flesh wounds. Anyway, I didn't remember that the PCP porn-vest guy was also named Worm."

"I guess that's because you were more preoccupied with me losing my wedding ring."

"Maybe."

Julia entered the room.

"I remember that the PCP porn-vest guy was named Worm, but Dad had more than flesh wounds, Mom. Remember, Dad was attacked by a giant metal decorative wall spoon that day that the housekeeper grabbed off the kitchen wall. I remember everything. I posted on my social media all about it."

"You did *what*?" Avery and Max screamed in unison.

"It was funny!"

"Julia, you know better! And, no, it wasn't at all funny."

"Dad, maybe the Worm you're looking for now is the same Worm as the PCP porn-vest guy, and he's just lost a whole lot of weight."

"No, the PCP porn-vest guy was twenty-three. Plus, I heard he died in prison."

"Oh, really? How did the PCP porn-vest Worm die in prison?"

"Eaten alive by bed bugs in a filthy jail cell. Supposedly."

"No!" Avery and Julia screamed in unison. "You cannot be serious!" Avery added.

"Avery, do you really think I would joke about something like that? There's a big lawsuit about it."

"I haven't heard about it."

"Fulton County, Georgia. You can look it up if you want. He was extradited there, and it essentially became a death sentence."

"Okay. Well, back to the doggie door Worm. Tell us more about him."

"He is sixty-four."

"Sixty-four!" Avery and Julia screamed in unison again.

"Okay. We're done. I don't need my family assisting me in solving crimes."

"That's one old criminal, Dad. Are you really going to let an old skinny guy going by the nickname Worm outsmart you?"

"Go away, Julia. You too, Your Honor."

Avery grinned. "I think Worm is my new favorite nickname of all of the criminal nicknames you've ever mentioned. Until today, Pop Freddy and Downtown Breezy were the clear front-runners. But there's just something about the name Worm."

"Mom, what about Thumper White? That meth lab Aryan Nation guy? Do you remember Thumper White?"

Max looked at Avery and Julia with exasperation.

"Okay. We're leaving now. Come on, Julia. Let's leave Dad alone."

Avery and Julia both went downstairs.

Max waited for them to get out of listening range and got on the phone and called his colleague Dave Baker.

"What's up? You working on Saturday mornings now?"

"Well, sort of. At home. I think I may have a location on Worm for us to check out."

"Which Worm?"

"The old gnarly guy Worm. The cat burglar."

"Oh, you mean the doggie door burglar. Not a cat burglar. You know that guy has hauled in hundreds of thousands of dollars' worth of people's loot now? He must be living large. Where do you think he is?"

"At the Dove Motel. West Dallas."

"Well, that's not exactly living large. It's also not a very peaceful place, despite its name."

"Yep. Meth lab central. My sources say he's in room forty-two."

"Your *sources*? What, you've got a criminal informant working the doggie door burglar case?"

"Dave, why don't we go over there and grab him? And we'll probably need backup. What do you say?"

"Backup? For old man Worm? What's he going to do? Gnaw on our arms with his gums?"

"Trust me. I'm heading down to the station. Clocking in for some overtime."

"You're obsessing about old man Worm, Max. But whatever. I'll clear it with Sarge and see you at the station in thirty."

Max and Dave were parked in a covert car in the Dove Motel parking lot an hour later, planning their door-knock strategy.

Suddenly, a strategy was no longer necessary. Old man Worm pulled up on his motor scooter with a knapsack slung over his back. His worm arm tattoo was fully visible.

Max and Dave got out and approached Worm.

Worm reacted by running from them. Not surprisingly, Worm didn't get very far.

As Max and Dave were cuffing Worm, a very heavyset redheaded woman in a bright yellow bathrobe came running out of room 42. At this point, marked police cars and uniformed officers were all over the place.

Worm yelled, “Misty, you stay out of this! Go back inside!”

Misty did not comply. She yelled in reply, “I ain’t got nothin’ to do with this, Officers. Nothin’. Nothin’. Here, take these!”

“These” were an armload of assault weapons of every make imaginable, wrapped in a white motel bath towel.

The unis, with arms drawn, descended on Misty.

Dave looked at Max. “She sort of looks like a human highlighter. Carrying a lot of guns.”

“What the hell do you mean, Dave?”

“That color she is wearing. Her robe is the color of a highlighter pen. Bright yellow.”

“That’s all you have to say right now?”

Dave grinned. “I know. I know. You are trying hard right now not to say, ‘I told you so.’ You’re wanting me to tell you that you were right about needing backup.”

“You’re damn right I was right. I was worried about those guns, Dave. I knew he had a meth lab in there and guns. And all kinds of bad dudes he deals with come and go from there all day long. And you, grasshopper, were only worried about old man Worm gumming you to death.”

“You’re calling me grasshopper. You’re the grasshopper.”

“I’m a wise old badass, Dave.”

“Sure. A regular profile in badassery.”

“Whatever.” Max and Dave fist-pumped each other and got into their covert car. The covert car was “burned” now, as the cops say when criminals have likely spotted it, so they would be taking it to the city impound and would find another car there to use for a while.

Before they took off, a young officer approached them and knocked on the door. Max rolled down the window. “What do you need, Rookie?”

“What am supposed to do with Misty? She’s not done anything that we know of. She’s asking us to take her to her brother’s trailer. He’s a groundskeeper down at the Mystic Spires Hotel and lives in an RV trailer out back.”

Max grinned. “Aldo Moses? That’s Misty the Human Highlighter’s brother? No kidding. I’ve talked to that guy before.”

The rookie looked at Max strangely. “Are you trying to warn me about something, Officer Lassiter? Is he a bad dude or something? I don’t understand.”

Max laughed. “No, I don’t think he’s a bad dude. But Rookie, you need to at least get a statement from Misty. She might not have been doing anything criminal, as she says, but she was staying with a guy who was making meth in their bathtub. Then you should ask Sarge if she is free to go.”

“Thanks, old man.”

“Don’t call me old man.”

Max rolled up the car window and grimaced at Dave. “Jeez. What do I do with Misty? *What do I do with Misty?* Can you believe that rookie asked us that? Since when do they let twelve-year-olds graduate from the police academy? He’s not even twelve. He’s a baby.”

“He’s not even a baby. He’s a fetus.”

“Yep. It’s time for us to retire, Dave.”

11

FLYNN FLETCHER, THE FLAMETHROWER

2012–2014

Genevieve Mesero was not married at the time of her tragic death. She had been divorced for a couple of years. Few people knew about her very brief, disastrous marriage. That was by design—Genevieve and her family tried to hide it, as best they could, from public consumption. It is, of course, well known that more women are killed by people who love them or once loved them than by strangers. Thus, spouses, partners, and exes are typically high on the list of suspects when a woman is murdered. Despite the veil of secrecy, the Dallas Police and true crime podcasters soon knew all about Flynn Fletcher. There was a heckuva lot to know.

Flynn Fletcher was a former personal injury lawyer in south New Jersey. During the heyday of his legal career, he went by the nickname the "Flamethrower." One had to wonder whether he had received advice from an advertising consultant to use that moniker or if he'd come up with it all on his own. Or maybe he had been tagged with that nickname by one of the "many satisfied clients" he professed to have or by the many intimidated defense lawyers whom he claimed to have 'whipped up on" in court.

After her marriage ended, Gigi had ultimately wondered about the genuineness of his "real" name Flynn Fletcher. She clearly should have wondered these things and run a background check on him before marrying him. Gigi could be such a kind, trusting soul—to a fault.

The Flamethrower had started out, after graduation from law school, suing Atlantic City casinos in slip-and-fall cases. Casinos have a lot of slip-and-fall cases. They are big properties, after all, and a lot of alcohol is consumed there. A lot of elderly people with health ailments also visit these properties at a time in life when they are retired and not able to partake in more physically challenging activities. The Flamethrower, who graduated very low in his class from a bottom-tier law school, smelled opportunity. He started a small law firm in a dreary strip shopping center in Atlantic City that grew at a very fast pace. He plastered the southern New Jersey geographical area with his billboards, the words THE FLAMETHROWER screaming out to passersby, along with an 800 number and a picture of him in jeans, a checkered blazer, and bolo tie, and wielding—yes—a large flamethrowing device spraying out burning fuel. He later progressed to late-night TV commercials after he had amassed a few settlements and court victories. Eventually, the Flamethrower had a firm of almost one hundred lawyers, which is quite large in the universe of personal injury law firms.

The Flamethrower's TV commercials went from tasteless and somewhat comical to more serious over time. He was originally cast as an arrogant, angry shouter (waving his flamethrower, of course) who was going to "get clients what they deserved" from the "greedy casinos who only cared about money and not their patrons' pain and suffering." Then, over time, the Flamethrower completely transformed himself in his TV commercials into a stern, subdued, quiet lawyer who never spoke but simply stood with his arms folded against a glass window inside a sleek skyscraper in a stuffy but elegant conference room. In the background, "a non-attorney paid spokesperson" would wax on about the greatness of Flynn Fletcher. Flynn Fletcher eventually stopped all references to the Flamethrower in his advertising and started dressing like a Wall Street lawyer in tailored gray conservative suits. His face stubble was gone, and he had a clean-shaven, grim countenance. He wore round, wire-framed glasses. He almost looked like he might have been generated by artificial intelligence—for example, if you instructed AI to create a picture of a respectable, trustworthy lawyer and suggested a twenty-first-century Atticus Finch as a template. Flynn Fletcher had no awards or honors to go with his new slick, loftier image. However, his commercials bragged of "Fletcher & Associates' numerous multimillion-dollar verdicts" and "satisfied clients," as well as being voted one of the "top places to work in south New Jersey."

One day, Flynn Fletcher got an offer he decided he could not refuse. The general counsel for a holding company of one of Atlantic City's biggest casinos called him. This particular holding company had been sued by Flynn several times. They called to make him a job offer. "Come to work on the dark side," the general counsel had joked. The holding company was based in Texas, although it had casinos in various parts of the U.S., including New Jersey, Las Vegas, Louisiana, and Mississippi. They would put Flynn in charge of the defense of all of their personal injury suits at all of their properties. But they had another project for him that was much larger in scope. They were beginning lobbying efforts in the State of Texas to try to get the legislature to legalize gambling—casinos in particular. They knew that Flynn Fletcher was not only born and raised in Central Texas but that he had an uncle in the Texas Legislature, Bo Fletcher, who had considerable clout. Flynn Fletcher took the job. A few years later, he was in Austin, Texas, wining and dining the most powerful Democrats and Republicans in both the Texas House and Senate. He was also investing in real property sites in Galveston, San Antonio, and other parts of the Texas Hill Country, where he speculated the demand for casinos would be at its highest.

Flynn Fletcher got a lot of help from his Uncle Bo and certain other Texas legislators. For many months in the 2010–2012 timeframe, it looked like casino gambling might pass. Flynn Fletcher not only bought lots of expensive meals and professional sports team tickets for people in high places, but he also hired one senator's girlfriend as a secretary, another one's son as a paid intern, and co-invested in certain land deals with yet another senator.

During this time frame, Flynn Fletcher met Gigi. Gigi was on a trip to the Texas Hill Country, helping her father close on a land deal there. The Meseros were purchasing the property that they would later develop into the Lacey Oaks Lodge between Austin and San Antonio. The Mesero family was making a significant footprint in the Lone Star State and nearby parts by this time. In addition to the Mystic Spires in Dallas, they developed and opened the Blue

Princess in Houston. They also had a property named the Emerald Belle in nearby New Orleans and the Hotel Salamanca in Santa Fe, New Mexico. At a post-closing dinner at the restaurant Jeffrey's in Austin, a few blocks south of the Capitol building, Gigi and her father were approached by Flynn Fletcher. Fletcher was drinking expensive bourbon at the bar, waiting on some other lobbyists to join him, and recognized Gigi's father from news articles he had read. Guillermo Mesero was, by this time, a very successful player in the real estate business and the hospitality industry in particular. He was a friend and a former business colleague of Carlos Slim, one of the world's richest men. This chance encounter seemed too good to be true.

Flynn Fletcher waited for the Mesero closing dinner to wind down. Then he made his move. He walked up to Mr. Mesero and confidently reached out his hand. "May I shake your hand, sir? I am a lawyer and real estate developer myself here in Texas, and I just want to say how much I admire you."

Guillermo and Gigi looked at Flynn Fletcher cautiously.

Guillermo then reached out his hand and warmly replied, "I am still not completely used to the friendly Texas ways. I have been here several years now, and I am never quite sure if someone is friend or foe. Especially when I am with one of my beautiful daughters. . . . It is a pleasure to make your acquaintance. Thank you for your kind words."

Fletcher Flynn turned to Gigi with a big smile and a cheesy wink. "So this is your daughter? You're a successful businessman, and you also have such a breathtaking daughter. What a lucky man you are. May I also shake your hand, Ms. Mesero?"

Gigi reluctantly stuck out her hand, and they shook.

"What brings the Meseros to Austin?"

"Business. Always business."

"Have you spent much time here?"

"Starting to spend more and more. And likely, I will be here a lot in the coming months. We are developing a new property close to Fredericksburg."

"How exciting. I have some properties in the Hill Country myself that I was thinking about developing as hotel properties or possibly as casinos if the Texas Legislature legalizes gambling soon, as I have been told it will. What would you think of that possibility? Would you view legalized gambling as a good thing or a bad thing for Texas?"

Guillermo was now getting uncomfortable at this stranger's quick familiarity with him and his daughter. "Oh, I don't know how I'd feel. But we need to get going. It was nice meeting you, sir."

With that, Guillermo and Gigi hurried toward the exit. As they did, Flynn Fletcher heard Guillermo make a phone call to his driver. He requested he pick them up so they could retire to the Four Seasons Hotel and call it a night.

The next morning, Gigi went for a run on the shady trails around the Four Seasons and Lady Bird Lake. When she came back into the lobby to grab some orange juice and a newspaper, Flynn Fletcher was seated in an area near a fireplace, drinking coffee. Gigi spotted him across the way, and he quickly waved at her. He then motioned for her to come over to him. She hesitated and then approached.

He stood up when she reached his table. "Fancy meeting you here! I guess you and your father are also staying here. It's my favorite hotel in Austin, but of course, it's not as nice as a Mesero hotel."

Gigi smiled.

"Please, will you join me for breakfast?"

"Oh, I am a mess. I need a shower after my long run. I really shouldn't."

"You look beautiful. You are the most stunning woman in this whole state. I would be honored to have someone to visit with. All I meet here in this town are politicians and lobbyists. I crave being around normal people."

"I thought you said last night that you are a lawyer and real estate developer."

"Well, that's true. But I'm doing a little bit of lobbying right now, too, while the legislature is in session. Hoping the lobbying gig will be finished soon."

Over the next several months, Fletcher showered Gigi with attention and gifts. In six months, the two were married. Gigi's father was less than thrilled. Her sister was horrified. None of them knew about Flynn Fletcher's prior life as the south New Jersey Flamethrower. But, even without that past, he still seemed like a somewhat sleazy, no-name lawyer turned real estate developer turned casino industry lobbyist. At the very least, Flynn Fletcher was not a serious person. He was not worthy of Gigi Mesero.

Flynn Fletcher naturally thought he had struck gold. He now had the clout he needed for the lobbying he was doing. He had married into the prominent Mesero family. He regularly implied to folks at the Texas Capitol that the Meseros were supportive of his lobbying efforts and would invest millions into casinos in Texas if the legislature legalized gambling. He suggested that this is what had prompted the Meseros to buy land in the Hill Country—they were hedging their bets, so to speak, that they could develop the newly purchased property into a casino. And all the surrounding land in the area would be worth a fortune—including the land that he and certain senators had recently purchased.

Unfortunately for Flynn Fletcher, most members of the Texas legislature cared more about their conservative constituency than a bunch of casino lobbyists waving cash and other graft their way. Texas never legalized gambling. Most thought it never would. And Flynn Fletcher and several members of the Texas House and Senate eventually got indicted by a Travis County grand jury for various forms of bribery and public corruption.

Gigi Mesero nearly had a nervous breakdown after this scandal. Ironically, the only thing that kept her sanity were her twin stepchildren. As it turned out, Flynn had eighteen-year-old twins, Finn and Frances, who were delightful despite their father's deficiencies. They attended the University of Texas.

Gigi filed for divorce less than two years after she met Flynn Fletcher.

Guillermo died a week after she filed for divorce. The Mesero patriarch had been diagnosed with pancreatic cancer just three months earlier that moved swiftly. The Meseros were Catholic. It was during her father's funeral mass that Gigi had the idea to try to obtain an annulment of her marriage. She knew that this would be her father's preferred result for this ugly stain on her life. And it was during this process of investigating the viability of an annulment that her family lawyer informed Gigi that Flynn Fletcher had been a law school near-flunky who once advertised himself as the Flamethrower. Gigi wondered if this hidden fact might help her case for an annulment. Maybe they could make an argument that Flynn had essentially hidden his true character from Gigi. Committed fraud through concealment of important facts? Flynn was a con man who conned her and her family. Gigi had always assumed Flynn was a respected real estate attorney. This had to be grounds for declaring the marriage null and void!

The Mesero family lawyer wasn't an expert in Catholic Canon law, but he was fairly certain that there would need to be an undisclosed prior criminal record for this strategy to prevail. Concealing the fact that he was a personal injury lawyer specializing in suing casinos—even one with a really horrific nickname—was probably not going to be enough to declare the marriage null and void.

Soon, Gigi gave up on the annulment process, feeling defeated and full of shame. She decided that a quick, quiet divorce from the Flamethrower was the best she could try to accomplish. A divorce—rather than an annulment—would simply have to be her punishment for allowing herself to be wooed by such a loser.

A HORSE NAMED REGRET

AUGUST 2016, FOUR MONTHS BEFORE GIGI MESERO'S MURDER

"What are you doing, Gigi?"

Valentina had just walked into Gigi's office behind the front desk area at the Mystic Spires. Gigi was adjusting a large, gold-framed oil painting of a regal, chestnut-colored horse with a wide, white stripe down her face.

"I'm hanging my new artwork. It was a gift from my friend Tanner. Isn't she beautiful?"

Valentina looked at the painting with a critical eye.

"So, Tanner is giving you expensive gifts now? How does his wife feel about that? And where does he get the money?"

"Oh, Valentina. He's just a great friend. I'm friends with his wife, too. She's not jealous or anything. Do you know who the horse is in this painting?"

"No, Gigi. I have no idea. Wait. Secretariat? Seabiscuit? Man o' War?"

"Do you want to keep guessing? I'll give you a clue. Your guesses are the wrong gender."

"Gigi, I have no idea. I don't share this newfound love of horses that you seem to have developed since meeting Tanner."

"Valentina, it's not a newfound love. I have always loved horses. Like Mom did, you know that. I'm just finally making time for them in my life. Don't discourage me."

Valentina walked closer to the painting. There was a brass plate on the bottom of the frame that read Regret. Valentina frowned. "Regret? Is there some deep meaning there that I don't understand?"

Gigi smiled. "You better believe there is. So, when I went to the Kentucky Derby this year with the Swensons, we happened to tour the museum at Churchill Downs." As Gigi talked, she moved to her desk and picked up a framed photograph of herself with the Tanners in which both of the women were wearing large, pretty hats and beautiful dresses and drinking mint juleps. Gigi continued. "When I was there, I learned about this little filly racehorse named Regret. She is my new hero. Tanner remembered how much I loved learning about her and found this painting of her. It's the sweetest gift I have ever gotten from anyone."

"So, what's the story with her name?" Valentina picked up the photograph of Gigi with the Swensons at the derby. She noticed Mrs. Swenson did not look as perky and cheerful as Gigi.

"Well, you may or may not know that the Kentucky Derby has historically been dominated by young male horses. Colts. There's actually a special race for young female horses, the fillies, on the Friday before the Kentucky Derby called the Kentucky Oaks. But the Kentucky Derby is technically gender-neutral, and fillies can qualify for and race in the Derby. In fact, something amazing happened in the year 1915. This little filly named Regret won the derby and won big! In the whole history of the derby—which dates back to 1875, by the way—only three female horses have won—the other two being Genuine Risk in 1980, and Winning Colors in '88."

"You still didn't answer my question about why the name Regret."

"I'm getting to that. The horse was born in the spring of 1912 in New Jersey at the Brookdale Farm to an owner named Harry Payne Whitney—Payne, as he was called. He was the son of a prominent New Yorker named William C. Whitney and was married to Gertrude Vanderbilt, the eldest daughter of Cornelius Vanderbilt. Payne received a substantial inheritance, and he invested in thoroughbreds, among other things. Over his life he was the breeder of something like two hundred champion horses. So he bred together a strong stallion—a sire—named Broomstick and a dame that was a great mare named Jersey Lightning. The offspring was Regret. The story is that upon Regret's birth, Payne was very disappointed because he had hoped for a male horse to be born of this great parentage. So Payne named the baby horse—the foal—Regret, to reflect his depressed mood at her birth."

"Are you about to tell me that the horse flipped the script on her owner by going on to win the Kentucky Derby?"

"Pretty much. Yes. Regret was entered in the Kentucky Derby three years later, after some success racing as a 'juvenile,' and she became the first female to win the derby. She led the race from start to finish and crossed the finish line as a two-length winner. And in another twist of fate, 1915 was the year of the Triple Crown fillies, with another girl named Rhine Maiden winning the Preakness. Regret did not run in the Preakness. Anyway, Regret's victory brought significant attention to the Kentucky Derby, and some say it was a turning point in elevating the race's popularity."

"Thank you, Wikipedia." Valentina's snarky comment dampened Gigi's enthusiasm just a bit. Valentina could tell Gigi was a little hurt. "Seriously, I guess that's a pretty good story, Gigi."

"Yeah. Apparently, Regret's trainer was pretty dubious about her chances in the derby, even though Regret was unbeaten in previous races. The train ride from New Jersey to Louisville upset the horse. She went off her usual feeding habits in Louisville. And she did not perform well on the track in the days before the race. Meanwhile, news of the lone filly in the race spread and attracted an overflow crowd of forty-nine thousand at the race. With all this pressure, when the flag dropped on race day, Regret shot out like a cannon billet, taking an immediate lead. A colt named Pebbles, her archrival in earlier juvenile races, chased her throughout, but she never let him catch her, beating him by two lengths. Twenty-nine fillies had competed in the derby in the forty years before Regret, but none of them had managed to be victorious or capture the attention of Regret. Here's the best part. Payne was quoted as saying after the race: 'Isn't she the prettiest filly you ever saw? You know, this is the greatest race in America at present.'"

Valentina laughed. "Hmmm. His tone really changed from the negative one he had on the day she was born when he named her, huh? I'm sure the purse money he won had nothing to do with it."

Gigi smiled. “This little filly was selected as Horse of the Year.”

Valentina sat down on Gigi’s cushy leather sofa. “I feel like I need a shot of good Kentucky Bourbon after that story. Got any?”

Gigi chuckled. “You know I do. Always.”

“So, why are male racehorses so much more successful than females?”

“Just like humans, I suppose. Male horses are typically slightly bigger and, therefore, a little stronger than females. The males also tend to be more muscular, with their necks being curved and stronger than females. At least in the case of stallions—the older male horses—on average, experts say they tend to be around thirty percent faster than mares—the older female horses.”

“So, Gigi. What is this about? You like the horse because she was a female for whom expectations were low, and she defied those expectations and left the males in her dust? Or is it mainly about her name and how a person who is the subject of disappointment can turn that situation around into something positive?”

“Valentina, you nailed it. Maybe you just understand me better than anyone. Now, and forever, any time I hear the word ‘regret,’ I’m going to think of this awesome horse and how she overcame the stigma of her name and the expectations of her owner, brought joy to a cheering crowd, and added to the prestige of one of America’s greatest sporting events. And I will have this painting here to always remind me.”

Valentina sighed. “Gigi, you’ve had a great life for the most part. We all make mistakes. You have really turned things around since divorcing Flynn. Don’t feel like you need to make radical changes to your life simply because of some regrets.”

“Valentina, I think I am going to walk away from all of this soon. Maybe I will sell my half interest in Belleza Mistica. Blake says he could help with that. Or at least get an appraisal done, so maybe you could consider just buying me out if you don’t want a new partner. Maybe I’ll just raise horses or develop my property up in Kentucky and be a one-property gal from now on. I don’t enjoy this complicated, massive business the way Dad did. I am trying to talk Tanner into joining me in that endeavor.”

“Gigi, you need to slow down. This is crazy talk.”

“Oh, Valentina. It’s just something I’m pondering. It may go nowhere. You know how I can get on some days.”

"Don't let yourself be manipulated by other people, Gigi."

"No one is manipulating me."

Gigi went to the bar cart in her office and poured two glasses of Blanton's and handed one glass to Valentina. Gigi clicked Valentina's glass and said, "Cheers. Here's to a horse named Regret. And also cheers to my great sister, who is always looking out for me."

"Cheers. May we both have no regrets."

13

CARTEL FAMILY

PRESENT DAY

It was an interesting sight to behold on a cold December morning standing in a check-in line at Prague's Václav Havel Airport. A beautiful, middle-aged Latina rapidly firing off commands to those around her in Spanish. Beautiful? Well, beauty is, of course, subjective, and hers was not a natural kind of beauty—at least not at this point in her life. The woman had surgically enhanced breasts and buttocks, with a tight, winter-white sweater and spandex pants to ensure that the enhancements were noticed and appreciated. Her fur-trimmed ski boots were surely not the most comfortable choice of footwear for air travel, but they were stylish. Like much of the rest of her body, her bright red lips had likely received cosmetic treatments, which had achieved an inhuman amount of plump and pout. Her eyelashes were black and velvety and measured around a half inch in length, top and bottom. Her silky black hair glistened and bounced as she busily pivoted from examining her cell phone to checking her makeup in a rhinestone-studded makeup case to occasionally opening and adjusting suitcase items.

There was a man with her who appeared to be around the same age—perhaps a husband or maybe a boyfriend. His primary role at the moment was interacting with the British Airways attendant regarding their ten carry-on bags. In addition to these, many carry-ons were surrounding them, most of which were Louis Vuitton.

Then there were the three children who were with them—probably ages eight to twelve. Hers only? His? Theirs? Hard to tell. The only thing certain was that the surgically enhanced woman was utterly uninterested in them and was constantly shooing them away from her. In fact, they almost seemed to disgust her.

It was a bit of a spectacle. The long line of weary travelers was fixated on the woman. Surely, someone in the line was secretly recording a TikTok video. Avery darted her eyes to make sure her kids weren't. The family's check-in process seemed to take an eternity. Granted, it takes an eternity for every airport traveler these days. It's as if the airline attendants are going through firewalls at the Pentagon. The clicking and clicking and clicking on their computers seemed interminable. What were they to do?

Baba Jo, Avery's mother-in-law, looked quizzically at Avery, and Avery, in turn, looked wearily at Max. "What could possibly be taking so long? Don't get me wrong. This is all very entertaining for sure."

"Cartel," Max uttered rather matter-of-factly.

"I knew it!" Baba Jo muttered. Like Avery, she had learned a few things from her police officer son over the years.

"What?" Avery replied with a wrinkled forehead.

"They're cartel, if you're wondering. Or at least he is."

"Oh my God, Max. Are you profiling people?" Avery constantly felt it was her duty to be her retired cop-husband's civil rights monitor.

Max rolled his eyes, and so did Baba Jo.

"Maybe," Max said. "But see their Aeromexico tags on their luggage?" Max nodded his head in the direction of the flashy, stylish woman, who was now fussing at one of the children for hovering too close to her.

"No. I just see Louis Vuitton. Louis Vuitton everywhere. Like they bought out an entire Louis Vuitton boutique."

"They may have," Max replied.

"Look, Mom. I see the woman that y'all are talking about has some shopping bags from Baden-Baden, my favorite European spa town!" Julia chimed in.

"Yes, sweetie. She has lots of shopping bags. And how does my young daughter have a 'favorite European spa town'?" Avery asked, using air quotes. "It's not like you've been to twenty of them."

Avery turned back to Max. "Back to your profiling. Why are you suspecting that he or they are cartel members?"

"I'm not suspecting, actually. I know. He is. His nickname is Worm. Sinaloa cartel. I knew I recognized him, and I just went back through my phone and found an old BOLO alert on him."

"You still get BOLO alerts?"

"Hey, you never know when I might come out of retirement or need the info for my current insurance company investigator job."

Julia chimed in. "Oh my gosh, Mom. Another criminal named Worm. Sweet!"

"Julia, quiet! They'll hear you. And surely your father is joking."

"Oh no, I'm not. El Gusano. 'The Worm.' That's who that is. He is a lieutenant, so to speak, for a big-time drug lord. I guess he's not quite high up enough in their ranks to take one of their private planes. Or it wasn't available during the holidays." Max grinned.

"Stop it, Max. Honestly, sometimes I don't know when you're joking or being serious. But really. What do you think might be stuffed in all of those bags? Something illegal? Drugs? Or was this just a family vacation, and they shopped a lot? And what are you going to do about all of this, Max?"

Baba Jo looked at her son judgmentally, as though she also expected him to somehow intervene in all this.

"What am I going to do about this? I'm going to mind my own business, Avery. That's what I'm going to do. What do you think I'm going to do? Show him my retired Dallas Police Department badge and arrest him myself right here in the Prague airport?"

"No, but I mean, shouldn't you call up Interpol or something? Is he wanted internationally? An international fugitive?"

"Oh, yeah. I forgot, Avery. I have Interpol on my phone's speed dial! I'll summon up an extraction team right now. Why didn't I think of that?"

Avery sighed. "Don't be a smart-ass, Max. Can't you call Dave Baker or one of your former colleagues back home or something? Tell them that you have eyes right now on a wanted Sinaloan cartel member and tell them to get on it. You can't just let this man slip back into Mexico. I'm guessing he's responsible for many people's deaths, right?"

"Avery, chill. Even cartel members are entitled to a little quality R&R with their families."

"Are you kidding me? Is he wanted for murder?! Multiple murders? Heinous murders? Tell me!"

"Shhh. Watch this. Quiet."

At that moment, a group of men in uniforms approached the cartel family. Speaking in English, they began, "Excuse me, Mr. Diaz. I need to speak with you privately. Can you and your family come this way?"

Suddenly there was active discussion among the family in Spanish. But the Worm—El Gusano—could see resistance was futile. Anyway, he no doubt had an army of lawyers available here in the Czech Republic, in Mexico, and in many parts in between. Maybe even in Baden-Baden. El Gusano looked cool as a cucumber, as if he had been through similar events in the past, and this would only be a minor inconvenience and delay.

Max, Avery, the kids, and Baba Jo stood in silence for several moments after the cartel family was escorted away to parts unknown. Everyone in the airport check-in line stood in silence as well. It was rather a lot to take in at 7:30 in the morning.

Suddenly, Julia spoke. "Dad, did you text one of your law enforcement buddies back home and somehow make that all happen just now? Are you going to get credit for that arrest?"

"Oh my gosh, Max! Who do these kids think you are?"

"Apparently, a badass. Maybe you had them convinced from your questions that I actually have a direct hotline to Interpol."

Avery rolled her eyes and began making sure that the kids had their passports ready to hand to the ticket agent. The Lassiter family was next in line.

"Mom, I wonder if the cartel family went to the Fabergé egg museum while they were in Baden-Baden," Julia whispered.

"Oh, honey, you *know* they did," Avery replied. "Maybe even pilfered an egg while they were there. By the way, Max, don't you think that the cartel woman looked a little like Valentina Mesero? I wonder what's ever become of Valentina Mesero. I heard she divorced a couple of years after her sister was murdered. You remember who I'm talking about, don't you? Gigi Mesero's sister? Remember, she was a suspect in Gigi's murder. Maybe Valentina hooked up with and married this El Gusano cartel guy after she sold the hotel empire."

"Really, Avery?" Max asked incredulously. "And maybe Valentina is now a hit woman for the Sinaloa cartel. Maybe she ran through all her millions or just got bored. Sheez."

Baba Jo weighed in. "Max, you joke, but I recently saw a reality TV show where something just like that happened. What was the name of that? Julia, do you remember? Didn't you watch it with me?"

Avery ignored Baba Jo's comment while Julia was engrossed in her phone.

"Max, I saw Valentina with Gigi once in Valencia, just a few months before Gigi was murdered. Just ask Julia. She was there. So was my sister."

Julia looked up. "It's true, Dad. We did." Julia stood with her hands on her hips in a rare moment of solidarity with her mother in an argument—or whatever this discussion was.

"Max, I'm telling you, even though she has visibly aged and apparently gotten lots of plastic surgery, I'm pretty sure that's Valentina Mesero. And Valentina had a Latin boyfriend with her that day we saw her in Valencia. He looked handsome and rich. Little did we know that it was El Gusano. Oh my God. Maybe he's being questioned about Gigi's murder right now—maybe they both are!"

Max looked down with embarrassment. He sometimes didn't know if Avery was joking or serious.

The Lassiter family stood in silence for a few moments. Baba Jo finally resumed the conversation.

"I wonder what plastic surgeon Valentina used. I have to admit she looks really good. I wouldn't mind getting pouty lips like hers. Wonder what that costs?" No one responded.

"Oh my gosh, Mom. I just Googled Valentina Mesero. Look at my phone. I think you're right. I think that was her. She's a social media influencer now. She has over a million followers. Here's a picture of her at a spa in Baden-Baden yesterday getting a facial."

Avery and Julia looked with satisfaction at Max.

Max sighed. "Well, that was kind of unexpected."

"Dad, wait until you hear this! When we were in Valencia, I saw Valentina and Gigi and their boyfriends buying NyQuil in a pharmacy."

Max looked incredulously again at them both.

Avery looked at Max. "It's true. She did. I remember it like it was yesterday."

"You remember everything like it was yesterday, Avery. It's the bane of my existence."

"Oh my gosh, Dad. I just know Valentina and El Gusano murdered Gigi Mesero. That's why they have been detained. Valentina and the Worm are being questioned about Gigi's murder right now, I bet. Should I go tell the Czech police about the NyQuil incident in Valencia?"

Max sighed and shook his head. "The NyQuil *incident*? Good grief. You girls wear me out. I need a vacation from my vacation."

14

SOON AFTER SEEING CARTEL FAMILY

PRESENT DAY

"Max, I've got an idea. I don't think you'll be crazy about it. But please keep an open mind."

Max looked at Avery with one of those looks that said, *Good grief. What are you about to suggest now?*

"Don't look at me that way. Just listen."

"I'm all ears."

"Well, you know how I've been wanting to invite all my present and current law clerks to a dinner party at our house? Well, I want to go ahead and plan something for next month.

"And why did you think I was going to have a negative reaction to that?"

"Well, I haven't gotten to the theme for it yet."

"Theme? Why does the dinner party have to have a theme?

"See, that's what I'm talking about. I knew you wouldn't want to have a theme."

"Well, what do you mean by 'theme'? I guess there could be good themes or lame themes. Like, I don't want to do costumes, so please don't suggest something lame like a costume party."

"No costumes. I want to do a mystery dinner theme."

"Ugh. Now *that's* what I mean by a lame theme. Those are so stupid. It takes like five minutes to figure out who did it in those games. They're never very challenging."

"Well, maybe not for you because you were a cop. But I didn't mean one of those mystery murder dinner games that you can buy."

"Then what do you mean?"

"We'll do the Genevieve Mesero murder."

"I have no idea what you're thinking here, Avery. That's an unsolved murder. It's not even for sure a murder—some people still think it might have been suicide. So there can't be a big reveal at the end. The murderer—assuming there was one—has never been identified. And how would you construct the script? I'm not going to go pull confidential case files. It wasn't even my case. I just did some intel the night of her death. I didn't even come up with much intel at that. Remember, the cameras at the hotel were not operational that night. Someone turned them off, or else it was just really bad-luck timing that the cameras happened to go out the night of her death."

"Good grief, Max. Of course, I wouldn't ask you to go look at old police files. I have this all figured out how it would work. I've done a lot of research during my spare time. I've come up with a list of the likely suspects for her murder. My idea is to give each law clerk an identity of one of the suspects, then they would research the person before coming to the party and then role-play them at the dinner party. And we can collectively come up with a vote of who did it."

Max looked at Avery with exasperation. He knew resistance was going to be futile. "For what purpose, Avery?"

"Why does it have to have a purpose? Max, I have been *obsessed* with this unsolved mystery ever since we saw Valentina Mesero and El Gusano in the Prague airport last month."

"Avery, you have no idea if that was actually Valentina Mesero."

"Oh, come on. You know it was. It had to be—although I cannot find anything on the internet about her hooking up with El Gusano Diaz or being detained in the Czech Republic. She probably just has a great publicist who kept that on the down-low."

"Well, why are you obsessing? I don't understand. There are, sadly, lots of unsolved murders and other horrible crimes out there. Why this one?"

"I know, Max. This one just bothers me so much. I have had so many legal interactions with the Mystic Spires Hotel and chance encounters with the Meseros over the years. Maybe that's why. And Gigi seemed like such a nice person. No one ever deserves what happened to her. But she had lost her mother at a young age. Then, her father. She apparently had a less-than-warm relationship with Valentina at times. She had no kids. She apparently had a string of poor relationships with men. She had questionable financial advisors who supposedly took advantage of her. I just want someone to care enough to bring her murderer to accountability. This is sort of my way of caring enough. Even if it leads to nothing. I just feel like she deserves it."

Max stared at Avery. "I can see that you have made up your mind on this. I'm not going to stand in your way. But just leave me out of the planning. At least the *theme* planning. I'll be happy to cook if you want."

"Paella and sangria, please? The kind of sangria made with cava, not red wine."

"You got it."

Avery went all-out on the murder mystery dinner. She sent out invitations the next week to her current and former law clerks and their significant others.

You Are Invited to

a Law Clerk
Murder Mystery Dinner

WHO

Genevieve Mesero
The murder victim.
To be played by Emma.

Blake Martin
The Finance Bro.
To be played by Rick.

Clarice Fleming
The victim's best friend.
To be played by Carol.

Maddie Swenson
The cowboy's wife.
To be played by Catherine.

Valentina Mesero
The victim's sister.
To be played by Millicent.

Flynn Fletcher, the Flamethrower
The victim's ex-husband.
To be played by Ned.

Cort Daniel
Valentina's ex-husband; the victim's brother-in-law.
To be played by Tom.

WHERE

The Lassiter house

WHEN

March 15 at 7 p.m.

THEME

A cold case murder in Dallas, Texas

Date of crime:
December 29, 2016

Your task is to research Genevieve's death and your assigned character. There's plenty out there on the internet. You should prepare a biographical script and be ready to role-play your assigned character. Then, together, we will try to solve this murder mystery.

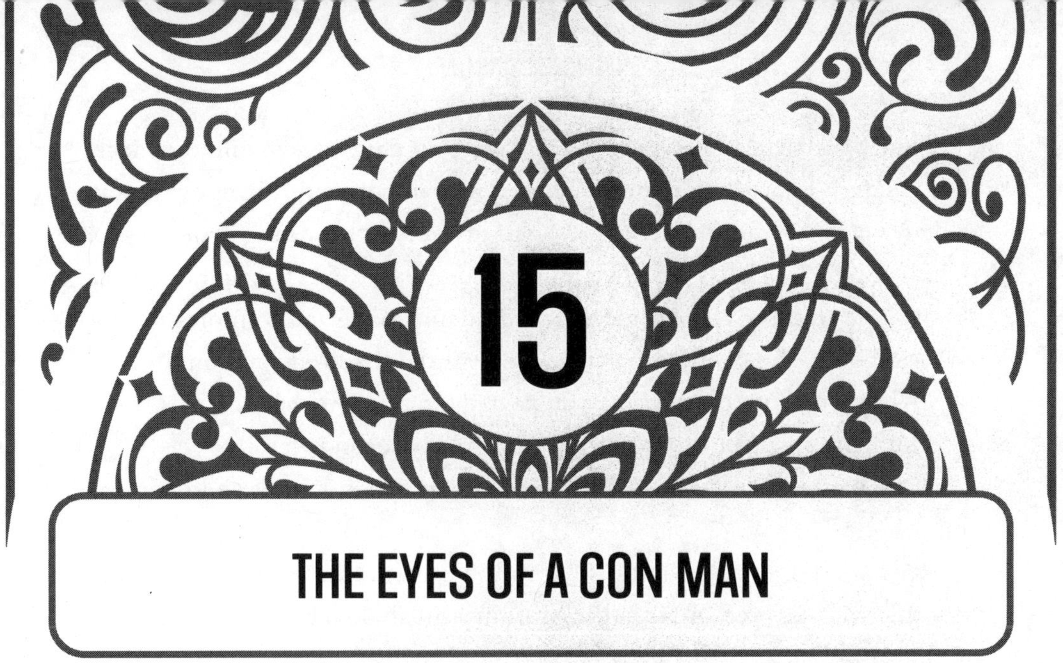

15

THE EYES OF A CON MAN

MAY 2014

"His eyes were emotive. It was the only thing about him that was. Everything else was still and calm. Unreadable."

Avery stopped and took a sip of her Cloudy Bay Sauvignon Blanc. She was having dinner at a legal conference with Judge Maria Ramos. On the menu was the usual unappetizing, bland rubber chicken and chewy, tasteless green beans.

Maria was looking quizzically at Avery as she sipped on her own prosecco.

"You know that saying that the eyes are the windows to the soul?" Avery continued. "I never really related to that concept. It sounds like a lovely poetic metaphor, maybe Shakespearean, but not really genuine or accurate. Anyone with experience in law enforcement or the justice system knows that there are liars and scammers out there whose eyes reveal nothing. Charmers with sparkling, glimmering eyes or even eyes that seem to be kind. Theirs are the windows to nothing. They certainly don't reveal their deceit or cunning cruelty or capacity to ruin lives."

Avery was describing a witness in one of her recent cases. Maria wasn't quite sure where this was all going.

"But back to his eyes. Maria, they were so dark brown, almost black. Dark, watery pools that somehow had a way of communicating with you. Pulling you into the moment. Eradicating every other thing around you. Hypnotizing? No. That's too silly a suggestion. His eyes felt like home. A place you wanted to stay. A frozen gaze that somehow made you comfortable, not awkward or fearful. Something you never wanted to look away from."

"Avery, snap out of it. I think you've had too much to drink."

"No, I haven't, Maria. I've barely touched my second glass."

"The waiter topped it off five minutes ago when you were looking at your phone."

"Oh. Well, I guess I should slow it down then. But I'm not tipsy. I tell you, this witness was smooth. I'm literally still shaken by his performance on the witness stand. He had a real way of drawing you in. I can see why so many investors fell for his lies. I wanted to believe everything the man said. Until I couldn't."

"When was the moment that you couldn't?"

"When he got gutted like a fish on cross-examination."

Maria chuckled. "Yeah. That happens sometimes. I used to love those moments when I was with the U.S. Attorney's office."

"Yes, because you were always the one gutting the fish. This was epic, Maria. It turns out this guy had scammed old people out of fifteen million dollars before someone got suspicious and talked to an attorney. He was selling alleged ownership interests in a wind farm that he was supposedly putting wind turbines on. Essentially selling unregistered securities to the public. He owned some land down in the Hill Country, and he swore it was legitimate. That his intentions were pure. He said he ultimately just couldn't get regulatory approval and nearby neighbors on board for the wind farm. He sounded somewhat believable, with his big brown eyes betraying nothing. Then this lawyer that my law clerks call Hardcore Hank whipped out an exhibit book full of bank statements that showed he spent all the old people's money on gambling, booze, and hookers."

"So cliché!"

"Yep. If I had a dime for every time we've both seen that fact pattern."

"Did you wonder why this guy's lawyer didn't tell him to take the Fifth? Why would he take the witness stand?"

"I don't know. This guy was even a lawyer by training himself, Maria! A lawyer turned real estate developer turned lobbyist turned scammer. I guess he thought he had the talent and intelligence to dance his way through any trouble on the witness stand."

"And, also, the pretty eyes to mesmerize."

"Hah, yeah. Those beautiful, brown con-man eyes. Sometimes, I wonder if I'm ever going to get used to this. The endless line of people willing to cheat others to get ahead. Do they think that they somehow deserve the fruits of their fraud? That it's every man, woman, and child on this planet for themselves? Is it a psychological disorder or are they just mean and evil? Do they degenerate from principled persons to corrupt ones, and if so, why?"

"And which of them can be rehabilitated?"

"Maria, you are so good. You always turn the negative to positive. Always forward-looking. Asking important questions like, can we fix these people? Can they find redemption? I tend to just let these awful people suffocate my spirit."

"No, you don't. You just hurt deeply for the people who are harmed by the charlatans. The victims. That's how people need for us to be. We are supposed to address injustices. We are supposed to feel the hurt. Would we be good at our jobs if we were indifferent to what we heard and saw in our cases? When we stop internalizing some of their pain, it's probably time to quit. It might not be what a psychologist would advise, but I say we have to internalize just a bit."

"Maria, like I said, you always stay positive. You listen to my irritable lamentations and just smile and have a comforting and optimistic response. I sometimes have trouble with finding the positive. Does that mean it's time to resign and give someone else a chance to judge? Sometimes, we judges lose our mojo. Despite what a lot of our colleagues might think, judges are not always like fine wine. We don't necessarily get better with age!"

"Just grumpier?"

"Maybe. I guess it's better to be a little grumpy and a little disillusioned, as opposed to corrupt."

"Corrupt? Oh God, please tell me we aren't going to start talking about dear old Judge Kurtz!"

"Aw, good old Kurtz. The horror! The horror!" Avery giggled.

"Oh, stop it, Avery, with your goofy literary references. I'm still furious about the whole Judge Kurtz thing. Don't even bring him up."

Both Avery and Maria were quiet for a few seconds as they sipped their drinks and checked their phones.

Maria broke the silence. "You know, one of Kurtz's law clerks used to have her groceries delivered to the courthouse. She even once had kitty litter delivered. It shut the whole courthouse down for an hour last year—because the court security officers naturally suspected the worst. No one had the nerve to tell her to stop because they were afraid of pissing off Kurtz."

"Maria, I thought we weren't talking about Kurtz anymore. Anyway, Mr. Brown Eyes. You know, I feel like I have seen that witness or heard about him somewhere."

"Oh, so we're back on the subject of that witness with the mesmerizing con-man eyes, are we?"

"I'm trying to remember his company's name. It was some generic name like Hill Country Wind, LLP. You know. One of those utterly unmemorable names that some uncreative corporate lawyer came up with. But wait! The guy's name was Fletcher. Flynn Fletcher. I'm just wondering if I've had him in some former lawsuit that escapes me."

"Hmm. Name doesn't ring any bells with me."

16

THE MISCREANT JURIST

2010–2013

Marlow Kurtz was a mere trial court judge. A public servant. Sure, he wielded some power. He was in a big city and drew some large, high-profile cases. But he displayed the self-assuredness and swagger of an Apollo astronaut from the 1970s without being nearly so accomplished or alluring. His self-esteem was absurdly inflated. This was typical of a lot of Texans. New Yorkers, too, sometimes. They both tend to think they live in the center of the universe, that the universe revolves around them, and everyone wants to be like them. Well, at least some of them. Certainly not all. Judge Kurtz had constructed an image of himself as brilliant, passionate, and hardworking. It was his own personal myth. And certain people—particularly, the lawyers who were profiting from his exuberant and unrestrained reign from the bench—fell hopelessly under his spell. He was more of a strategist than a jurist. He was creating a Field of Dreams of courts: if you build it, they will come. And lawyers did, from all over the country, due to accommodating, flexible venue statutes. What was wrong with that? Congress wrote the venue statutes. Lawyers have and will always take full advantage for the best interests of their clients.

Judge Kurtz was creating a business court where certain lawyers and clients seemed to get whatever they asked of him. And they often asked for extraordinary relief. He barely read their pleadings. He barely required notice to affected parties. His view of due process was not the same as other judges. Some people felt completely unnerved by him or at least ill at ease. What was really going on there? Something didn't feel quite right. But you better not question him or express any reservations. Things might not go well for you if you did.

Everything was all about Judge Kurtz, the charismatic demigod. He was fueled by attention. The more, the better. For him, it was not about the cases, the parties, or legal precedent. He loved and sought out publicity. He feigned compassion and empathy when it suited him. He pushed all acceptable boundaries when it came to fraternizing with lawyers who did business in his court—so much for the "lonely" life of a judge. He flirted with women, discarding appropriate norms. His behavior was calculated and extreme, clever and careful—except, ultimately, not careful enough.

Judge Marlow Kurtz was an imposter in a robe. He was not a brilliant and fair judge. And he was not simply an egomaniac who liked handling big cases and hanging out with powerful, rich lawyers. He was the Talented Mr. Ripley of jurists, playing a game. Quite a lucrative game, actually. He was pretending to be something he wasn't. Then there was the precipitous downfall. Well, not just that—his career ended in a ball of flames. Some of his improprieties were finally exposed. His eagerness to be the king of the bench had flowered into not just impropriety but criminality. His exposed misdeed—and certainly not his only one—was that he was "on the take" from certain lawyers—one, in particular, with whom he had a long-standing friendship. Flynn Fletcher. Judge Kurtz was quite insistent that he had done nothing wrong. But, of course, he had. He eventually resigned before being forced out, with an air of "I'm too good for all this."

And just like that, a collapse. The Field of Dreams imploded. The lawyers took their marbles and went to another spot. This spot—with Judge Kurtz gone and U.S. Attorneys snooping around—had become utterly inhospitable. Its secrets had been revealed. And, of course, everyone involved claimed to have known nothing.

Judge Marlow Kurtz was an arrogant criminal, an isolated figure. He was not representative of the rest of the profession. Truly he was not. Although some might beg to differ.

Somehow Kurtz and Fletcher spiraled into oblivion, unscathed. Sure, they did some things that might have made others go to jail. But they each had a knack for landing on their feet. It's almost like a gift or talent that some have. They both hightailed it out of Texas at some point and started anew somewhere else. Flynn Fletcher had supposedly moved to Louisiana for a while and was involved in new business ventures. Kurtz was rumored to be consulting with Fletcher in some capacity from a distant location—on some island, or perhaps an Asian enclave where digital nomads could work from afar without paying taxes. Their skill sets would serve them very well, no matter where they were or what they ended up doing.

17

THE MURDER MYSTERY DINNER PARTY, PART I—THE ENACTMENTS

PRESENT DAY

It was the night of the dinner party. All of Judge Lassiter's law clerk guests arrived, seemingly eager to role-play. They each took their assigned task very seriously, as they did everything in life. They were all young legal superstars. One by one, they each got up and read their script as follows, beginning with Emma, playing Gigi.

"I am Genevieve Mesero. Sadly, I am the subject of tonight's murder mystery.

"At the time of my death, December 29, 2016, I was a thirty-nine-year-old, dark-haired, brown-eyed beauty. A vivacious and wealthy Dallas socialite. I grew up in the Park Cities in Dallas and went to the University of Texas. I was a shy sorority girl and an Art History major. I loved horses.

"I had one sibling, my sister Valentina, who was two years younger than me. My father was a wealthy titan of the hospitality industry named Guillermo Mesero, who grew up in Mexico City and moved to Dallas as an adult. My mother, who died in a plane crash when I was only four years old, was a beautiful half-English, half-French woman who was an accomplished athlete and globetrotter. My father called her the Lioness, and her portrait hangs in all the Mesero hotel lobbies.

"My father had a fondness for travel. We traveled the world when I was a child and teenager. In addition to the Mystic Spires in Dallas, he owned hotels in Houston, the Blue Princess; New Orleans, the Emerald Belle Bed & Breakfast; Aspen, the Buttermilk Mountain Boutique; and Santa Fe, the Salamanca. He also owned properties in Latin America. He had started developing a property to be known as Lacey Oaks Lodge in the Texas Hill Country at the time of his death, but there had been significant setbacks getting it to completion. I and my sister Valentina would sometimes work at the Mystic Spires when we were teenagers, especially during summers when we were off from school. My sister and I inherited the whole company, Belleza Mistica, when my father died.

"A couple of years before my father's death, I married a man named Flynn Fletcher. It was a disastrous marriage and divorce. Suffice it to say I was single and living alone at the time of my death.

"Here is the moment you have all been waiting for: the details of my death. Although I was a Dallas Park Cities socialite, I eventually moved into a penthouse at the Mystic Spires to always be available to take care of business at the hotel. On December 29, 2016, the night of my death, I got home very late. It was a Saturday night and there was a party at the Dallas Country Club. It was fun and I was tired, but, as usual, I had trouble sleeping that night. I took some NyQuil cold medicine to help me sleep.

"At approximately two a.m., I called my sister Valentina in a panic to report that I could not breathe and felt terribly nauseous. When I called, Valentina's husband Cort answered her phone, and I mentioned to him that I had taken some NyQuil and thought I might be having a terrible reaction to it. Valentina and Cort lived about ten miles away, and Cort said they would rush right over to my penthouse. When they arrived, the doors to my penthouse were unlocked. My security alarm was not set. They rushed back to my bedroom, and they found me lifeless, lying on my king-sized bed. They called paramedics, who performed CPR, but I was declared dead at two forty-two a.m. Although everyone at first thought I died of natural causes, an autopsy about seven days later revealed that I died of strychnine poisoning. The bottle of NyQuil that I had taken was found in a drawer in a nightstand next to my bed; it was put in an evidence bag, along with other items by police, on the early morning of my death, but it had sat in an evidence room until after the autopsy. The bottle was tested after the autopsy, and, in fact, a very large amount of pure powder-form strychnine was found in it.

"Strychnine is a tough way to die. Usually, within fifteen minutes of ingestion, victims experience muscular twitching, followed by a sensation of suffocation and a sudden onset of massive convulsions. One's head and feet are bent backward in spasms, and one's face turns blue. Each convulsion is followed by a period of relaxation until the victim experiences the onset of the next convulsion. Death, ultimately caused by paralysis of the respiratory muscles, swiftly follows after three or four convulsions. After the FBI investigated and ruled out the possibility of product tampering with the NyQuil at either the manufacturing or sales chain level, and after Dallas police and a forensic psychologist ruled that suicide was improbable, my death was ruled a homicide. My killer has never been identified.

"Those who were close to me knew that I sometimes had trouble sleeping, and it was a regular habit of mine to take a dose of NyQuil to help me get to sleep. Strychnine is used in rat poisoning, but the type of strychnine used to kill rodents contains less than three percent strychnine. I was killed with an almost pure form of the poison, obtained legally only through chemical outlets to authorized buyers. Only about a hundred companies around the country use or sell strychnine, according to the Environmental Protection Agency. As a result, the poison is rarely seen in homicides. Apparently, it is also available in some college chemistry labs, and it is occasionally seen on the black market, where it may be added to cocaine or other illegal drugs to kill people.

One last odd fact: On the Monday before I died, a friend of mine from Highland Park called to check on me and said she had had a dream that I had been killed by two men. I had just laughed it off."

Emma sat down. "I'm done."

Everyone clapped with hesitation, not knowing if applause was appropriate. Emma had done a great job. But, of course, it seemed a little disrespectful to clap.

Avery broke in to alleviate the awkwardness. "Okay. That was pretty heavy. Who needs a break? Or a drink?"

"Let's keep going, Judge. I'm ready to go next."

"Okay, Millicent. Is everyone else good to keep going?" All nodded affirmatively. "Millicent, you're on."

Millicent stood up, adjusted her skirt, and took a deep breath before beginning.

"I am Valentina Mesero, Gigi's sister. Like Gigi, I am a dark-haired beauty. But I was never quite as pretty or beloved as her. In recent years, I have gotten out of the hotel business and become a social media influencer.

"Gigi and I were very close and, of course, business partners at our inherited hotel empire. The business was doing pretty well at the time of Gigi's death. Well, actually, we were struggling to get the Lacey Oaks Lodge in the Hill Country past the finish line. There had been construction delays and mistakes by subcontractors, permitting problems with local authorities, cost overruns, problems with our lenders, and a need for more financing. And the Mystic Spires needed a lot of repairs. The Emerald Belle in New Orleans had suffered severe damage during Hurricane Katrina and had never bounced back to its former self. But we were still making money overall with all of the properties combined. Some people thought I was jealous of Gigi, but that is not true. There was some friction because she knew I did not ever approve of her ex-husband, Flynn Fletcher, and she did not approve of my now ex-husband, Cort Daniel, either. Anyway, Gigi texted and called my cell phone at two a.m. that fateful night, and Cort heard and answered it—I was sound asleep. I knew immediately that something was horribly wrong when I woke up. I could overhear Gigi telling Cort that she thought she might be having a bad reaction to her NyQuil, and I immediately recognized that it would have been normal for her to have taken NyQuil before bedtime to help her sleep. Cort said she was practically incoherent and breathless on the phone, so we couldn't get much information from her. So, Cort and I rushed over to the Mystic Spires. I did not have a key to her penthouse, but the door was unlocked when we got there. Cort and I went inside and called Gigi's name.

"Gigi was lying unconscious on her bed in blue silk pajamas. I frantically called 911, and Cort began attending to Gigi but could not revive her. Cort said that he performed mouth-to-mouth resuscitation, and some green liquid had oozed from her mouth, but I did not actually witness this. To our shock, several days after her funeral, the autopsy revealed that Gigi had died of strychnine poisoning. At that point, there was some initial discussion of whether Gigi might have committed suicide. I knew that was impossible.

That was not in Gigi's nature. She was happy. There was no suicide note. And Gigi had recently purchased a cutting horse named Pillar for sixty-six thousand dollars that she was excited about and determined to ride in competitions. She had begun training with a horse trainer named Tanner Swenson in the town of Granbury, Texas, a few months back. She had already entered one competition and was making progress in the sport. She was talking about acquiring a one-hundred-acre ranch in Granbury where she would raise horses. She was talking about developing a property in Kentucky with a distillery where she would breed thoroughbreds. The day before her death she had made a down payment of ten thousand dollars on a mare she planned to breed. She was very excited about this new venture. And her alarm clock had been set the night before she died—presumably a sign that she intended to get up.

"As far as our relationship, it was good. It probably should be mentioned that we were supposed to get together in early January with our board of directors and discuss, essentially, a succession plan for our business in the event either one of us died. You see, after our father died, Gigi and I had entered into a "buy-sell agreement" with each other that worked as follows: Each sister owned a one-million-dollar life insurance policy on which the other sister was the sole beneficiary. If one of us died, under our agreement, the surviving sister was required to use the life insurance proceeds she received to buy out the dead sister's equity interest in the hotel business. This would leave the surviving sister as the sole owner of the hotel business, and the dead sister's heir or heirs would get the one million dollars of life insurance proceeds—as essentially their sale proceeds for what otherwise might have become their inherited interest in half the hotel business. For me, my sole heir was Cort. For Gigi, she had made her former stepchildren—Finn and Frances Fletcher—as her sole heirs. It seemed sort of ridiculous to me that she would make these kids her heirs because her marriage had been so short. But she loved those kids and felt sorry for them having such a bad dad.

"While the buy-sell arrangement was less than perfect, we figured that this was the simplest way to buy peace and keep the business within the family. If this all sounds strange for a couple of women who were only in their thirties, it really shouldn't. Because, sadly, I had cancer a few years before Gigi's death. My prognosis was initially bleak, but I was declared in remission later. When our father died, his personal affairs were a total mess—he neglected his personal financial affairs and put all his attention in the business. Gigi always said that she would never put our heirs—whomever they might turn out to be—through the trouble we went through after our father's death. In any event, when Gigi died, our discussion with our company board regarding proper succession plans had not begun. Therefore, upon Gigi's death, I received the one million dollars from her life insurance policy, then paid it over to Gigi's two stepchildren to buy out Gigi's half of the business—with me, then, becoming the sole owner of Belleza Mistica, LLC. The two stepchildren initially indicated that they, with the help of their father, were going to put up a fight and try to get Gigi's half of the business instead of the million dollars of life insurance proceeds. Greedy kids—considering that they were not her blood relatives, and their father was a total creep who had made Gigi's life miserable. I told them to back off, and they did.

"Anyway, it is regrettable that we never got to implement the succession plan. I am not entirely sure what Gigi had in mind, but I think her goal was to make sure that, if my cancer came back and I died, there was no chance that my half of the business would go to Cort. She did not even want him to get it for a split second. She, frankly, did not want to have to pay him a million dollars of life insurance proceeds to get it. But, as my will was currently drafted when she died, he would get everything I owned when I died. A lawyer said that this might override the buy-sell agreement. I admit that this would be Gigi's worst nightmare to share ownership of Belleza Mistica with Cort. She really hated Cort."

Millicent sat down.

The group was silent this time. The law clerks were rather impressed by Millicent's amazing research. It was no surprise to Avery. Amazing research was Milly's stock and trade.

"Gang, I am so impressed how seriously you all have taken this. This is really good. Shall we keep going?"

Tom jumped up. "I'm ready," he said. He glanced across his fellow dinner-party attendees and clarified, "I'm playing Cort."

"Well, let's go. Everyone, please feel free to go refresh your drinks at any time. Just as long as you plan to take an Uber home."

Tom got up with his script and dove right in.

"I am Cort Daniel, Valentina's ex-husband, and Gigi's former brother-in-law. Valentina and I divorced shortly after Gigi died, and our marriage was strained for a while before then. I received an undisclosed settlement when Valentina and I divorced. My whereabouts now are unknown.

"I was actually Valentina's second husband, and frankly, Gigi didn't like me much. She thought that I was not good enough for Valentina and had married her for her money. I am a few years younger than Valentina. I met Valentina when my landscaping maintenance company was doing some work for the Mystic Spires. I later started my own general construction business and used a lot of Valentina's money to finance it. My company didn't do a lot of business. I mostly hung out in an office at the Mystic Spires. I am a big-game hunter and had stuffed wildlife on display in my office at the hotel. I would tell people I had killed them on exotic hunting trips. Gigi hated them because she thought I was blowing Valentina's money on all of it. I was once accused many years ago of assaulting a girlfriend, and Gigi knew about it because she had a background investigation done on me. I am not sure if Gigi ever told Valentina about it. Kind of ironic that Gigi did a background investigation on me and not on that lousy Flynn Fletcher before marrying him.

"Anyway, on the night of Gigi's death, I woke up when I heard Valentina's phone going off. I answered it. It was Gigi in a panic, saying she was really sick. We, of course, rushed over to the Mystic Spires, which was not too far away. After rushing up to the penthouse and knocking furiously, we discovered that the door was unlocked. We found Gigi's lifeless body on her bed. I performed mouth-to-mouth resuscitation on her, and green liquid started oozing out of her mouth. The paramedics showed up soon and they likewise tried to revive Gigi, but it was no use. The medical examiner showed up, and at two forty-two a.m. she was declared dead.

"I remember noticing a table out on the balcony with two wineglasses and an empty bottle. The door to the balcony was wide open, which seemed odd for December. I didn't see any other signs of anyone else being there that night or of any foul play. Gigi had lots of valuable artwork and other expensive things in the house, and nothing seemed to be missing. I was eventually considered a person of interest in Gigi's death since people told police that Gigi hated me and also because I was the first person to actually see Gigi dead—well, along with Valentina. But I passed a lie detector test. Think about it. Why would I have given Gigi mouth-to-mouth resuscitation if I had poisoned her, since that would potentially put me at risk of getting dangerous poison in my mouth? And if I was guilty, why didn't I just dump out the bottle of NyQuil or hide it under my coat?

"Anyway, it's pretty ironic to me that Gigi thought her sister married a loser—me—when Gigi's own ex-husband was a horrible person who married Gigi for her money and family name and treated her like dirt."

Tom took a bow and sat down.

Avery stood up. "You are all master thespians. Okay, we are almost halfway through. Three characters down and four to go. Ned, we are ready for you now."

Ned stood up. He was a former hockey player and was tall and imposing.

"I am Flynn Fletcher, Gigi's ex-husband, to whom she was married for only a couple of years. Some people say that my and Gigi's short-lived marriage was volatile and an absolute disaster. That's probably a fair statement. Anyway, I turned out to rank very high on the murder suspect list.

"I am a Central Texas native who went out of state to college and law school—a bottom-tier law school. I practiced personal injury law in Atlantic City, New Jersey, after law school. I sued casinos in slip-and-fall cases, advertising myself as the Flamethrower."

Naturally, the law clerks laughed hysterically at this comment. Ned even found an old picture, which he held up for all to see, of Fletcher from those days brandishing a flame-spitting cannon.

Ned resumed. "I eventually morphed into a more suave-looking lawyer and went to work for the legal department of a casino. They transferred me to Texas, where they enlisted me to do lobbying work, trying to get the legislature to legalize casino gambling in Texas. I was not successful at that and would eventually be indicted on public corruption charges.

"I was fourteen years older than Gigi and gray-haired and handsome. We met in Austin when Gigi and her dad were in the early stages of working on the Lacey Oaks hotel development. I happened to own a couple of properties nearby that I hoped to develop if gambling was legalized. One of them was in La Grange, Texas, near the infamous old brothel that had notoriously been called the Chicken Ranch."

The law clerks did not react at all to this last bit of information. They were clueless as to the reference. Ned looked a bit disappointed.

Avery spoke up. "Max and I recognize that reference, Ned—oh, I mean Flynn."

Max started to hum the old ZZ Top song.

Ned smiled and continued. "Anyway, I talked to Gigi about some of the art and memorabilia I had already acquired for my future properties and was storing in a warehouse. There was a lot of Texas history antiquities, oil paintings, framed documents, and other memorabilia from the Mexican–American war, and I thought the Meseros might even think that some of it was a good fit for their Texas properties. I had approached Gigi's father, but he seemed insulted by my suggestion. He never really warmed up to me. Gigi and I eventually married after only a few months of dating. My kids really liked her, and she adored them. She often visited them in Austin, taking them to sporting events and nice dinners and furnishing their apartments.

"One reason that Gigi and I had a volatile marriage was because, frankly, I admit I had a gambling problem. After my lobbying efforts concluded in Austin, I moved to Dallas with Gigi. While in Dallas, I frequently spent long days at the country club at the card tables, participating in high-stakes poker and gin rummy games with rich and powerful men there. I would bet big and lose big. These habits naturally made Gigi very uncomfortable. Gigi had moved to her penthouse at the Mystic Spires before we married to be accessible twenty-four seven. She wanted to stay there after we married, and it made me miserable—I told people at the country club that living in that place was dreadful.

"People say I was emotionally cruel to Gigi and that it started right after we got married. I went from being charming to being a jerk. Anyway, we eventually divorced. The tipping point to our troubles was when the IRS tried to attach her separate property and earnings to pay my tax debts of about six hundred thousand dollars. The IRS was not successful, partly because we had a prenuptial agreement that ultimately prevented the IRS from getting her assets. I, by the way, had unsuccessfully tried to get the prenuptial agreement declared null and void.

"Here is why I was high on the suspect list: I was involved in lots of litigation at the time of Gigi's death. There was civil litigation involving a suspicious fire at a building in Galveston, Texas, where I had been hoping to open a casino and was storing the Texana artifacts that I had purchased for that intended project. The insurance company suspected arson and would not pay for my losses at the building. They suspected arson because I was in deep financial trouble at the time of the fire. I countersued the insurance company for insurance coverage, and things got very ugly. Also, I had a criminal trial coming up in the near future regarding the bribery and public corruption indictment in Austin."

Ned paused and took a drink of a beer. He scanned the group dramatically. "Okay, this is about to get good. Listen up closely."

The Lassiters' two Cavalier King Charles Spaniels, Jake and Finley, bolted up from their naps near the fireplace as though they were fully participating in the sleuthing exercise.

"It turns out that Gigi had been deposed as a witness for both of Flynn Fletcher's ongoing legal matters. She had said some very damaging things in her depositions, such as that the contents of Flynn's Galveston building had been removed and were not being stored there when the fire happened."

"You've slipped into third person, Ned!" Millicent corrected him.

"Oh, sorry. Right. As I was saying, Gigi basically suggested I, Flynn, was committing insurance fraud. She also corroborated the Travis County prosecutors' theories that I was giving all sorts of gifts and cash to government officials and legislators to bribe them into supporting casinos in Texas. The lawyers involved had talked to her many times. I ended up being considered a suspect in Gigi's murder, based on a theory that I supposedly didn't want her to testify at my upcoming trials.

"Also, I was considered a suspect after police learned that Gigi had gotten a restraining order against me because I was supposedly harassing her and stalking her after our divorce. Gigi even told her sister and friends that I had been watching her in the days before her death. She said that she was afraid to testify against me in the upcoming trials. It's true, I called her on several occasions, talking about her testimony that she would give; she was telling people I was pressuring her to change her testimony, and she told me that she was going to tell the truth.

"Oh, and one more thing. After her death, I refused to take a polygraph test."

Ned sat down.

This was getting really interesting.

Avery stood up again to play master of ceremonies. "Bravo. This is so riveting. And, you know, I'm thinking I may have had Flynn Fletcher testify in one of my cases several years ago. It was a case involving a wind turbine farm. Or a fake wind turbine farm, actually. I never made the connection until this moment!"

Everyone in the room looked intently at Avery.

"Oh, never mind. Maybe I have him mixed up with someone else. Let's do three more characters and then let's stop for dinner and discuss all this. Rick? Are you ready?"

Rick stood up.

Rick was perfect for the part of Blake Martin, the Finance Bro—except that he was a little *too* likable and handsome. Rick had been a financial advisor for a while before law school. He knew the type of person he was playing perfectly. He had also been a Marine, so he was not pretend-macho, but the real thing.

"My name is Blake Martin. I earned an MBA from Wharton. I grew up in Westport, Connecticut. I was rich as hell. I had an apartment in Manhattan, a house in the Hamptons, and vacation spots all over the world. I spent most of my career as an investment banker in the distressed business space. I was introduced to Gigi Mesero after her father died, and she and her sister took over the hotel business. They ran that puppy into the ground. Gigi called me in to fix up the mess. I wasn't sure the juice was worth the squeeze if you know what I mean, but I felt sorry for her and took on the project. I had gotten it back into decent shape by the time she died.

I dated Gigi for a while during all that time, but it was no big deal. It wasn't serious. She was sort of the needy type, and I just couldn't deal with that, you know? We had some good times, but I wasn't ready to settle down, and neither was she. Shame what happened to her, but I was really not close enough to have much more to say. I was at my Lake Como house thousands of miles away when Gigi was murdered. If that's not an alibi, then I don't know what would be. And what would be my motive? Like I said earlier, I was rich as hell. And I was not ready to settle down.

"So, why do I keep talking in the past tense? Because I am dead. It turns out that I was in town when the Mystic Spires burned to the ground in late

2018. I went over to the scene a couple of days after the fire and was looking around in the ashes. I had briefly dated a bookkeeper who worked at the hotel, Marcey Davis. Marcey had died before I started dating Gigi of some sort of fast-developing stomach flu. Marcey just went home from work and died one night. It was crazy sudden. Anyway, I had been looking in the ashes from the fire for a safe that Marcey had told me about once. Apparently, Gigi kept some valuables in it, and I thought she may have stashed in there some of the jewelry I gave her. I gave Gigi some expensive stuff. Anyway, the police saw me and questioned me. I told them the truth about it. Then, a couple of nights later, I'm driving in Uptown Dallas, and I see the cops following me. I don't know why, but I sped up instead of pulling over. We got into a high-speed chase. Then, I crashed my Porsche. Wiped out. Hit a tree. Dead at the scene."

Rick sat down.

"You guys are just amazing," Avery said. "Have I had too much to drink, or is this really as good as I think it is? Next, Catherine."

Catherine stood up and calmly unfolded her script before her.

"My name is Maddie Swenson. I am married to a man named Tanner Swenson, a tall and stunningly handsome cowboy. We live on a large ranch outside of Granbury, Texas, about ninety minutes out of Dallas–Fort Worth. My husband Tanner was training Gigi with riding and raising horses in the several months before she died. In fact, we boarded a horse that Gigi had recently purchased named Pillar.

"My husband Tanner and I fell under some suspicion regarding Gigi's death. We had cashed a check that Gigi gave us shortly before she died. Gigi had written in the date on the check—December 28, 2016, which was the day before her death—and she had signed the check and made a notation that read "saddle." But she had left the check amount blank. I added the word "and fees" next to the word "saddle" and filled in the amount on the check: twenty thousand dollars. So, what was the big deal? Well, apparently, the day before she died, Gigi had asked her best friend and financial manager, Clarice Fleming, to liquidate some of Gigi's personal assets in order to make five hundred thousand dollars available for Gigi to close on her new ranch that she was about to buy outside of Granbury, near us, whose sale closing would be happening soon—the closing had been moved up two weeks. When Clarice

Fleming asked if there were any outstanding checks on her account that she would need to cover before transferring out the five hundred thousand dollars, Gigi did not mention a large check to us. The honest truth is that Gigi was in the process of buying several horses through us, and she was paying us for the horses' boarding and training. She had spent most of the month of November living with us, working on her riding. Gigi gave me that check and simply told me to add up what she owed us for several months' boarding and horse-contest entry fees. So, I filled in twenty thousand dollars. Gigi probably didn't even remember giving us that check when her financial manager asked her, and she certainly didn't know the amount of it yet. Jeez, it was only twenty thousand dollars. That amount of money was nothing to Gigi.

"Gigi's sister and best friend grew even more suspicious when they learned that Gigi's expensive new horses were in my and my husband's names. The horses were in our names for a good reason: Gigi said that she didn't want her loser brother-in-law, Cort Daniel, to get his hands on them in case something happened to her.

"The fact is, Tanner and I had become a major part of Gigi's life in the year before her death. Gigi was always saying, and told several friends, that if she 'could find a man like Tanner Swenson, she'd marry him.' I know that Gigi's sister wondered if I or Tanner had a motive to kill Gigi. They think maybe Tanner had fallen in love with Gigi, and he had been rebuffed by her. And they think I may have been jealous of her. The detectives have suggested that poison has sometimes been used by horse breeders. But Tanner and I took a polygraph, and we both passed."

Catherine blew a kiss to everyone, giggled, and sat down.

Avery faked a drum roll. "Okay. Here goes. Carol, you're last. Is this going to be the best?"

Carol stood up. "I don't know. We'll see."

Carol held out her script, then winked at the audience with a smile.

"I am Clarice Fleming, Gigi's best friend and personal financial planner. We went to the University of Texas together and have been friends ever since."

Carol put her right hand up in the Hook 'em Horns sign, and the other law clerks hissed.

"Hey, I'm just role-playing here! Anyway, I am not under any suspicion, but I am going to share some random facts that you may find interesting.

For one thing, Gigi told me and several other friends that a marriage counselor described Flynn Fletcher as a 'sociopath' and that she should get out of the marriage immediately. Gigi told me and other friends that Flynn told her once, while they were still married, that he knew people from his south New Jersey days who could get 'anything done,' including having someone 'snuffed out.' Also, one hotel employee said that Gigi often asked him to cash checks for as much as ten thousand dollars for Flynn. Gigi told the employee that these were his gambling winnings, which didn't really make any sense. Also, people at the country club reported that, at some point, there was a 'murder mystery party' given by Flynn after Gigi's death. Flynn was the only one who guessed the murderer had hired a hitman, according to members who were there.

"With regard to Gigi's brother-in-law, Cort Daniel, there was a tape of the 911 emergency phone call that Valentina had made when they discovered Gigi's dead body. While talking to the dispatcher, Valentina can be heard saying in the background, 'You have to blow into her mouth,' as if urgently trying to instruct Cort how to perform CPR. Also, the paramedics reported that Gigi regurgitated 'large amounts of clear liquid' the instant that they began their CPR. One paramedic told the investigating police detective, 'Nobody performed CPR on this woman.'

"Neither of Gigi's former stepchildren—Flynn Fletcher's children—fell under any serious suspicion; they were both on a college ski trip the night of the death—although a detective did wonder if a college student might be able to obtain strychnine from a college chemistry lab. In any event, on the day after Gigi's death, her stepdaughter reported receiving a strange phone call from a woman. The caller insisted that she had to speak with Gigi, and the stepdaughter told the caller that her stepmother had passed away. The caller then supposedly said, 'Good, I wanted her dead.'

"Fast forward to when the Mystic Spires burned to the ground twenty-three months after Gigi's death. Arson investigators ruled that the fire had started at an electrical box. It was determined to be accidental, although the insurance company challenged that for a significant amount of time. The property insurance company eventually paid out thirty million dollars of proceeds, not nearly enough to replace the hotel, which would cost about fifty million to rebuild. Valentina, upon receiving the insurance money, immediately sold the land and decided not to rebuild the Mystic Spires. And Valentina thereafter sold all of Belleza Mistica to a private equity company for an undisclosed price believed to be only in the tens of millions of dollars—far less than its value when Guillermo died; this was partly because the company had suffered a substantial decline in value after COVID-19 devastated the hospitality industry. So poor Valentina, the grieving sister, made tens of millions of dollars before disappearing into cyberspace to become a social media influencer."

Catherine then pulled out her phone, showing a picture of Valentina from her Instagram account, sunbathing in a yellow bikini on a beach at some exotic location. Catherine curtseyed and said, "That's it."

Avery started clapping and said, "Another round of applause for all of you. Now let's go eat paella and sort through all of this!"

"Hang on. Hang on." Max entered the front of the room. "I have a character to present as well."

"What? No way. My fuddy-duddy husband?"

"I know. He's going to play the investigating officer that night! This will be great!" Millicent said. Not a bad theory on her part.

"Nope, I am going to be a recent ex-boyfriend of Genevieve."

"What? There was another one besides the Finance Bro?"

"Yep. His name was Darrin Albright. May I?"

"Sure. We can't wait."

Max surprised Avery by pulling out a square of paper from his back pocket and unfolding it, his face fixed in stoic focus.

"My name is Darrin Albright. I dated Gigi for a while after her divorce from Flynn Fletcher but before Finance Bro. We stopped dating several months before Gigi died. She broke up with me, and I was upset but not upset enough to kill her.

"I fell under suspicion after a Dallas Police detective got an anonymous phone call from a male caller who said, 'Did you know that Darrin Albright dated Veronica Dew?' Who, you ask, was Veronica Dew? She was a beautiful, sexy Fort Worth woman who had, sometime earlier, been found dead by her sister in her bedroom, stabbed through the neck. It was true that I dated Veronica Dew. I admit that it sounds a bit suspicious—that I have had two former girlfriends who were the victims of murder and happened to both be found in their bedroom by their sisters.

"Anyway, I owned a company called Albright Chemical Company. I grew up in Fort Worth near TCU, playing football for the Country Day private school and later TCU, where I took a lot of chemistry courses. My father was a butcher who ran a meat-processing plant. My chemical company was essentially a restroom-sanitizing service that made lots of money. We didn't use strychnine in my business for anything. But investigators wondered if I knew something about strychnine from my knowledge of chemistry, and they also discovered that I happened to make a purchase in the fall of 2016 at the only outlet that sells strychnine in Dallas. But strychnine was not one of the chemicals listed on the receipt of what I purchased.

I met Gigi in 2012 at the Dallas Country Club, where she was on the arm of Flynn Fletcher but was not yet married to him. I admit I was attracted to her and later asked Flynn where things stood between them. Flynn told me to back off—that she was not available. After Gigi and Flynn later married, they, of course, quickly divorced, and I then asked Gigi out. We discovered we both had a love for horses, which was a bond. Gigi ended the relationship because I eventually wanted to marry her. But, after her disastrous marriage to Flynn Fletcher, Gigi said she would never again tie the knot. Anyway, I took and passed a polygraph test."

Max began handing something out to the guests.

"What's this, Max?"

"It's like I have heard you say a thousand times, Judge Lassiter. You should always create a timeline when you are trying to sort through a problem. We always did the same thing in police work. So, I created a timeline."

"Oh my gosh. This is fantastic. But we need to eat. Let's bring our timelines to the dinner table."

The written timeline that Max had prepared was as follows:

- Jan. 2013: Flynn first meets Gigi.
- Apr. 2013: Flynn and Gigi marry.
- June 2013: Cort Daniel and Valentina marry.
- Feb. 2014: Fire destroys Flynn's Galveston building.
- June 2014: Flynn is indicted in Travis County, Texas, for bribery and corruption.
- July 2014: Valentina is diagnosed with cancer.

- Sept. 2014: Gigi and Flynn separate; Guillermo Mesero dies; Gigi's divorce is final by December.
- Jan. 2015: Marcey Davis (Gigi's bookkeeper) dies mysteriously at age 26.
- Feb. 2015: Gigi and Valentina enter into their buy-sell agreement.
- Fall 2015: Gigi gives damaging depositions in connection with Flynn's insurance lawsuit and criminal matters.
- Apr. 2016: Valentina's cancer goes into remission. Gigi, determined to keep her brother-in-law Cort from ever owning any portion of her assets, begins discussing making changes to the buy-sell agreement she had with Valentina.
- Dec. 2016: Gigi's murder.
- Jan. 2017: A scheduled meeting to discuss succession plans with Belleza Mistica board and changing the buy-sell agreement between Gigi and Valentina.
- Jan. 2017: Flynn's insurance fraud trial regarding the Galveston warehouse fire is scheduled. Gigi receives a witness subpoena.
- Feb. 2017: Flynn Fletcher's criminal trial is set to begin. Gigi is expected to be called by the prosecution as a witness.
- Nov. 2018: The Mystic Spires Hotel burns to the ground. Arson investigators ultimately rule that the fire had started at an electrical box; the insurance pays $30 million, not nearly enough to replace the hotel, which would cost about $50 million to rebuild. Valentina pockets the money and sells the land where the Mystic Spires Hotel used to sit. Valentina then sells Belleza Mistica to a private equity fund.
- 2019: Flynn's trials continue through 2020. Flynn ultimately is acquitted in his criminal trial and also prevails in his civil trial with the insurance company.
- ?: No one remembers the exact date, but several people at the Dallas Country Club report that, at some point, there was a "murder mystery party" given by Flynn after Gigi's death. "Flynn was the only one who guessed the murderer had hired a hit man," says one friend.
- 2021: Valentina hires a well-known private detective to try to determine who killed Gigi. Murder remains unsolved.

The dinner guests, at first, quietly loaded up their plates with paella and filled their glasses with sangria. Spanish food was the Lassiters' favorite. After a while, people began excited discussions. At first, it all seemed overwhelming. A beautiful woman's life had been lost. Multiple lives, actually, had been lost in this whole saga. No one could lose sight of that. But Gigi deserved some dignity in this situation. Her family and friends did. Unsolved murders mean loved ones suffer forever from not knowing.

Jake and Finley wandered from guest to guest, hoping for table scraps to be dropped or offered.

After twenty minutes or so of eating and drinking and banter, Avery called everyone back to the murder mystery circle in the living room.

18

THE MURDER MYSTERY DINNER PARTY, PART II—THE THEORIES

PRESENT DAY

"Okay. Now that we have had fuel for our brains, who wants to offer a theory?"

The group was silent at first.

"I can't believe this group is quiet."

Millicent spoke up. "I kind of feel like we should save a lot of time and just let Max give us his theories."

Max put down his drink. "I really don't know any more than any of you. Just to be clear, I barely had any involvement the night of the murder. I wasn't on the investigative team. I just helped, mostly on the perimeter of the property, for an hour or so, and I looked at some nearby cameras and license plates on nearby traffic. And I chatted a little with a groundskeeper. But I will tell you what I think you already know. Motive and opportunity are your two primary focuses. I'd start by talking about people's motives."

Emma spoke up. "The problem here is that a lot of people had a motive. Pretty much everyone we have discussed tonight. Except maybe Finance Bro. But who had the strongest motive?"

"I think Valentina did," Tom waded in. "Who knows how the succession planning meeting in just a few weeks was going to turn out? What if the Belleza Mistica board of directors had something completely different in mind than either one of the surviving sisters taking over if one of them died? And Valentina was jealous of her sister. Lots of people apparently said that. And Valentina was probably afraid that her sister might do something crazy like suggest bringing in her stepchildren to the business soon. They were soon going to finish college. Gigi adored them enough to name them her heirs, even with their creepy father."

Avery stepped in. "Does anyone except me think it is unfathomable to imagine a sister killing her own sister—especially when they each had no living parents or other siblings or children of their own? The two had to be very close even if they bickered some. No way Valentina killed her sister."

Max chuckled. "Famous last words. No one can ever believe there is such evil in the world until you see it every single day of your life."

"God, you're so cynical."

"It's called reality, dear."

"Well, maybe Valentina and Cort did it working together," Ned suggested. "I mean, it's so crazy that they get a phone call in the middle of the night, and Gigi sounds like she is dying, and they don't immediately call 911. They take their own sweet time getting over there. And it just so happens that the door is unlocked, and all the cameras at the hotel are down. And some newbie employee is working at the front desk. Valentina could have easily arranged all of that. And they could have easily staged the scene on the balcony to make it look like Gigi had a visitor that night. And, of course, Valentina knew about Gigi's NyQuil habit."

Rick chimed in. "Maybe it was Cort alone. His marriage with Valentina was on the rocks. He no doubt knew about the upcoming board meeting to discuss succession plans. Did he really think he was going to be part of that succession plan? He knew Valentina was soon going to dump him. Maybe he thought that if he killed Gigi, that would delay the board meeting for a while. Valentina, under the still-effective buy-sell agreement, would get the whole company at Gigi's death, and maybe he could either patch things up with Valentina or at least get a chunk of the company in a divorce with her. Maybe he was hoping, meanwhile, Valentina's cancer might come back."

"Oh my God. This is so terrible!" Catherine exclaimed. "I admit, all of this sounds plausible. But for crying out loud, what about that scumbag the Flamethrower? He is clearly the most obvious suspect here. He was about to go to trial in January for insurance fraud and then again in February for felony bribery. Gigi was going to be the star witness. Flynn was literally at risk of going to prison if Gigi testified. And Gigi had to get temporary restraining orders against him at some point! And their marriage counselor said Flynn was a sociopath! And that whole craziness about the murder mystery party he threw at the Dallas Country Club! It's like he was taunting the whole world: 'Look, ha ha ha, I did it, and no one can prove it.' And he once told Gigi that he knew people who could get things done—he probably knew New Jersey mobsters from his Atlantic City days. And let's not forget that his children were going to get a million dollars in insurance proceeds out of her death. He probably even brought them into it."

Max broke his silence. "I have to throw in some food for thought here. Does a man kill with poison?"

Avery spoke up. "Maybe he does if he knows his ex-wife takes a swig of NyQuil every night at bedtime."

"I'm just throwing this out there. Men—especially if there is anger involved—usually resort to more violent means to kill. And as far as him saying he knew people who could get things done, you don't need a hit man to slip poison into a bottle. I would bet my money that all of the men who are suspects here—Flynn, Cort, Finance Bro, the ex-boyfriend Darrin—are not the killer. Death by poison seems more like a woman-type of thing."

Millicent replied, "So I bet you think it was Maddie Swenson. She thought her husband and Gigi were falling in love. Gigi was about to move out to Granbury, where she would be close to Tanner. She was doing horse business with him. Training for horse-riding competitions with him. And remember how Gigi's stepdaughter said she got a phone call from a woman saying she was trying to reach Gigi? And when the stepdaughter said Gigi was dead, the woman said, 'Good, I'm glad she's dead.'"

"How do we know the stepdaughter didn't make that up?" Max countered. "The stepdaughter had a million-dollar motive to kill step-mommy dearest!"

Avery held up a hand. "Jeez, Louise. Y'all are really getting riled up here. Maybe we should shift the conversation to opportunity. Several folks had motive, but did several folks have opportunity?" Avery asked. "Who might have gotten this pure powder form of strychnine? Maddie? Did she have access to this in connection with their ranch and the horses? Putting out poison to kill rats and other critters that might bother the horses?"

"Yes," agreed Millicent, "and let's not forget that Maddie no doubt knew about Gigi's NyQuil habit since Gigi stayed out at the Swenson ranch frequently. She could have slipped the strychnine in Gigi's NyQuil bottle when Gigi was out riding horses with Tanner."

"I'm still not convinced it was a woman. What about that dude, Darrin Albright?" Emma asked. "I'm really suspicious of him since Max brought him up. He was probably obsessed with Gigi. He wanted to marry her, but she rebuffed him. And he owned a chemical company. And he had some other girlfriend a while back who was found dead in her bedroom. What are the odds of that?"

"What about Blake, the Finance Bro?" Catherine offered. Why hasn't anyone suggested he did it? The police had to be following him for some reason when he crashed in his Porsche. And isn't anyone bothered that he briefly dated that twenty-six-year-old bookkeeper at the Mystic Spires, and she supposedly died of a flu bug after leaving work there? And what was Finance Bro really looking for in the ashes after the hotel burned in 2018?"

Max spoke up. "Now, do you all understand why this has never been solved?" I'm not sure I have ever heard of a case where there were so many possible suspects. And, of course, the murder happened at an old property where the technology wasn't that great, as far as cameras and an up-and-running security system."

Rick spoke up. "Should we be discussing the groundskeeper?"

"Nobody was assigned to be the groundskeeper tonight," Millicent replied. "I assume that's for good reason."

"Who are y'all talking about?" Ned asked.

"Well, in my research, I discovered that there was a groundskeeper or handyman at the Mystic Spires named Aldo Moses," explained Rick. "Kind of a gnarly old guy. He lived in an aluminum trailer behind the hotel. He was passed out drunk or high or both the night of the murder. He was questioned, but no one had much concern about him. But I read that he had a criminal background and had worked for the Tiger King at one time."

"The Tiger King?!" everyone exclaimed at once.

Max interrupted. "I actually talked to Aldo Moses on the perimeter the night of the murder. He was never under any serious suspicion. I don't remember anything about a Tiger King connection. And don't know why that would be relevant."

"Well, I don't know for sure if it was the Tiger King he worked for. I just heard on a podcast that Aldo Moses once worked at a big-cat private zoo up in Oklahoma, and I assumed it was the one that the Tiger King guy famously owned. Anyway, between that experience and him being a groundskeeper at the Mystic Spires, I figure he would have had access to rat poison at least and maybe pure powder strychnine."

"Carol, what do you say about all this? You've been kind of quiet." Avery poured Carol a cup of coffee that she had just brewed.

"Well, I have an idea. Why don't we ask AI?"

"What?"

"Why don't we ask one of the open-source artificial intelligence platforms who it thinks murdered Gigi Mesero? You know, use its algorithms to come up with the most likely theory. It could be interesting."

Everyone fell silent.

The murder mystery dinner concluded at midnight, with a decision that the group would perhaps have another gathering in a month or so after they had cogitated on all the information and theories. They would also ponder whether to ask some type of artificial intelligence product who "it" thought killed Gigi Mesero. A legal game, of sorts, of "what do analytics say?"

Avery had very mixed feelings about this. Would it sort of be fun? A total waste of time that was not fun? An insult to Gigi's memory and those who loved her? Maybe this had already gone too far. The best-laid plans, and all.

19

WHAT DOES AI SAY?

PRESENT DAY

It was the night of the reunion of the murder mystery dinner group. Avery's law clerks would be over at 8 p.m., this time for dessert and coffee only. And, of course, the main event: consultation with artificial intelligence to see who it identified as Genevieve Mesero's killer.

Avery was quiet as she put out her china dessert plates and cups.

"You're so quiet, Avery. I can tell something's bothering you."

"Oh, I guess I'm just regretting a little bit that I agreed to this exercise tonight. I am feeling really worried about how it might go."

"What's the big deal? You can use this exercise to teach a lesson maybe to the law clerks, don't you think?"

"I suppose. I'm probably going to get philosophical, though."

"Why philosophical?"

"I don't know. I'm just bothered by our human nature. Our natural tendency to want to trust things or believe things that might not be real."

Max looked perplexed as he brought out the silver stemware.

Avery continued. "Some things aren't real. And yet, humans want to believe. It starts when we are small children with things like Santa Claus and the Easter Bunny. Then, at some point, we grow up, but it continues. So much of the world is fake right now. Illusions. Mirages. And, still, we want to believe."

"Good grief, Avery. Where are you going with this? It's just technology we are talking about. It's just the newest step in our ever-growing digital world. You have to view it all with a grain of salt. Artificial intelligence might give humans new ideas that they would not otherwise think of on their own. Hopefully it makes us smarter and more efficient about some things. But you obviously cannot assume what it generates is always true. When I was a cop, I looked on suspects' Facebook and Instagram accounts and the like. But you never know for sure what's real and what's total bullshit on there. It's just a possible clue. A digital clue. And, as for AI, facial recognition software is one common type out there. But I never could have gotten a warrant solely based on something, say, that facial recognition software showed. It would just be a starting place to follow up on. I mean, everyone knows that the facial recognition algorithms are sometimes faulty. It's not infallible but can be useful to get cops to maybe examine something they would not have otherwise examined. That can be a good thing."

"I know what you're saying," Avery said, "but I'm not sure every cop out there is following that protocol. And I guess I am thinking bigger picture here than just using AI in connection with legal investigations and proceedings. It's just everything now. It just feels like technology has brought fakeness in the world to a whole new level. Social media posts that are disingenuous with heavily edited photos. It's like a simulated existence people have created for themselves. And people are getting 'bots,' rather than real people, as 'followers' on people's social media. I've read about 'click farms' of low-paid workers in places like Indonesia and Thailand that are clicking away all day on rows of mobile phones with stacks of SIM cards, creating false 'likes' or false reviews of products and are fraudulently simulating traffic to websites to make things 'go viral.' We've even had situations in the courts of ChatGPT or other generative artificial intelligence platforms writing legal briefs with fake cases—we call them 'hallucinated' cases. How is that happening? People use fake backgrounds on Zoom calls. God knows what people are doing half the time with those virtual reality headsets. I sometimes read news stories that you can tell are generated at least with partial help from AI and are full of mistakes and misinformation. And deep fakes where people are being blackmailed. Even Wikipedia is sometimes fake—it can be edited anonymously by anyone—why would anyone trust that?"

"Oh my God. Avery, calm down. You are on a roll, there. You are going down a lot of different paths here. Let's go back to the topic at hand."

"I don't think I got off topic!"

"You sort of did. Look, in legal cases, there have always been reliability risks—way before AI or other technology came on the scene. Eyewitnesses sometimes have faulty eyesight or weak memories. They might be easily persuaded by a convincing lawyer or their own personal biases. Humans sometimes make mistakes. And, sadly, sometimes humans lie. This all can lead to wrongful suspect identification and convictions. You've said it a thousand times."

"But I guess I just feel like we can ferret those situations out, at least a lot of the time. But with technology—with all of these AI tools—are we prone to trust it more than humans in crime-solving and a court of law? Maybe more than we should? And are we at risk of delegating our own thinking—our own reasoning process? Are we going to just, more and more, defer to the machines to sort through a set of facts or legal issues to tell us what to think? That scares me to death. What about *cogito ergo sum*? 'I think, therefore I am'? We are facing an existential threat here, maybe. If we begin delegating our thinking, we are done."

"Wow. Avery, as usual, you are maybe overthinking this all a little too much. This is just a silly party. I mean, I shouldn't say silly because a human being died, and that's the subject that we're dealing with. But I suggest you just relax and try to have fun. As I said, maybe there will be a way to work some teaching moments into this with your law clerks."

Avery shook her head.

An hour later, everyone had arrived. Everyone had their desserts and coffee or espresso. No one wanted decaf. It might be a late night.

"Okay. How are we going to do this?" Avery asked. She had never experimented with an AI platform, but, of course, all of the law clerks had.

Millicent stood up. “Well, we’ve all talked through this. We each have different AI platforms on our devices.”

Avery interrupted, “You’re talking about your personal devices, not work devices, right?”

“Of course, Judge.”

“I had to ask.”

“So, we have a list of questions. Starting with ‘Who killed Genevieve Mesero?’ Shall I go first?”

“Go for it.”

Millicent set up her laptop so that it would connect with the Lassiters’ large TV screen in their living room. When she typed the question into the query box, several long paragraphs immediately appeared on the screen.

> Genevieve ‘Gigi’ Mesero (born December 1, 1977) was an American hotel heiress, the daughter of wealthy Mexican American business tycoon Guillermo Mesero and his French English wife Vivienne. She died from ingestion of strychnine poison contained in a bottle of cold medicine on December 29, 2016. The death, which occurred at her penthouse suite at the former Mystic Spires Hotel in Dallas, Texas, was ruled a homicide, but no arrest was ever made, and the murder remains an unsolved mystery. Suspects included:
>
> Flynn Fletcher, her ex-husband who was a lawyer, lobbyist, and real estate developer and was embroiled in litigation involving insurance fraud and charges of bribery and corruption at the time of Mesero’s death. Fletcher’s two young adult children (Gigi’s stepchildren) received $1 million of life insurance proceeds as a result of Gigi’s death.
>
> Valentina and Cort Daniel, her sister and brother-in-law who discovered her body. Valentina became the sole owner of the Mesero hotel empire, Belleza Mistica, after Gigi’s death. She sold Belleza Mistica a few years later after the Mystic Spires Hotel burned in what was first believed to be arson but was later ruled to be accidental.

Blake Martin, a recent boyfriend who was a wealthy investment banker and financial advisor to Belleza Mistica. He came under suspicion when he was caught sifting through the ashes at the grounds of the Mystic Spires after it burned in November 2018. He said he was looking for a safe with jewelry he had given Gigi. He once dated a bookkeeper at the Mystic Spires who died in 2015 of mysterious causes. He was killed in a car crash in late 2018 while being followed by police.

That was all.

"That's it?" Avery exclaimed. "That didn't tell us anything we didn't know already! And what about Maddie Swenson? It said nothing about her being a suspect! It also said nothing about that boyfriend—what was his name—the one that owned a chemical company and had another girlfriend once found dead in her bedroom."

"Darrin Albright!" everyone yelled simultaneously.

"Yeah. Darrin Albright. I am not very impressed at all. I mean, I'm kind of impressed with how fast it spits out an answer. But beyond that, I'm not impressed."

"Judge, we are not finished," Tom reminded. "We have other AI platforms to try. And we have more questions to ask."

"Well, okay. Someone go next."

One by one, the law clerks set up their laptops and connected them to the big-screen TV. And one by one, there was a similar result when the different platforms were asked "Who killed Genevieve Mesero?" Only one of five mentioned Maddie Swenson (erroneously stating that she was from Grapevine, Texas, not Granbury, Texas, and referring to her as a business partner of Gigi's—which was not entirely accurate), and none mentioned Darrin Albright.

Carol started round two. "I suggest we now ask the AI platforms, 'What are some alternative theories for who killed Genevieve Mesero?'"

Everyone agreed that this was a good next step. Avery, by this time, had both her dogs in her chair with her, fighting for lap space. She was considering getting up to spike her coffee with some Baileys Irish Cream.

Carol then typed in the question regarding alternative theories about the murder.

Once again, the AI platform spit out multiple paragraphs with lightning speed. In addition to the prior answers regarding Flynn Fletcher, Valentina and Cort Daniel, and Blake Martin, this time there was a paragraph about Darrin Albright and Gigi's stepchildren Finn and Frances Fletcher—with regard to the latter, pointing out that they realized one million dollars of life insurance proceeds. But to everyone's amazement, the following paragraph was generated:

> Misty Moses, a former housekeeper at the Mystic Spires Hotel, whose brother Aldo Moses was the groundskeeper who lived in a trailer on the premises, is considered a suspect by some. Misty occasionally lived in Aldo Moses's trailer and is believed to have been on site the night of the murder. She had access to the penthouse and had recently been fired by Genevieve Mesero after certain of her jewelry went missing, and Misty was suspected. Misty Moses had prior convictions in Oklahoma for misdemeanor theft. She also occasionally resided with a longtime boyfriend who spent much of his life in the penitentiary for numerous felonies. While her prints were all over Mesero's penthouse, this alone was inconclusive since she had regular access to it during her time as a housekeeper.

The law clerks sat in stunned silence.

Max broke the silence. "Misty? *Misty?* Old man Worm's Misty? The human highlighter? No way."

Avery and the clerks looked at Max. "Are you going to explain?"

"I once arrested Misty Moses's boyfriend, Worm."

"Oh my God. Here we go again with another criminal named Worm," Avery said, with the law clerks staring at her in confusion. "Don't ask, kids. There's something about criminals and the nickname Worm."

Max continued. "I can't remember when, exactly, but it was a few weeks or months after Gigi was murdered. I arrested a gnarly old-man-burglar who was breaking into mansions in North Dallas, crawling through doggie doors and stealing people blind. He was also making meth in a bathtub at the Dove Motel in West Dallas and trafficking guns out of there. I remember Misty was his girlfriend. She came running out of the motel room in this bright yellow bathrobe and gave the Worm up."

"Thus, the human highlighter reference," Ned commented.

Avery rolled her eyes in embarrassment.

Max continued. "And I remember Misty wanted the cops to take her to her brother's trailer at the Mystic Spires. I remember thinking that was crazy because I had met her brother, Aldo Moses, out at his RV trailer the night of the Mesero murder. I never heard a word about Misty being a suspect in Mesero's case. Not one word. That's crazy. There's no way she did it. No way, I tell you. Where is AI even getting this information? It's not like police records are public information. I don't know if this is one of those crazy hallucinations you read about or what. I tell you, even if someone within the police department suspected her, their records could not find themselves into an AI platform."

"Well, sir, you did tell us that it was likely a woman, in your opinion," Emma commented. "Poison would be the murder tool of a woman, not a man. And there are leaks and hacks of nonpublic records all the time."

One by one, the law clerks set up their laptops to do their individual searches of different AI platforms. All of the platforms, except for one, generated a similar response when asked for alternative theories as to who killed Gigi Mesero. In other words, all but one came up with the Misty Moses theory.

Max was visibly annoyed. "There is no way Misty Moses did this. I know in my gut this is crazy."

"How do you know in your gut, Max?" Avery said. "I mean, remember, I was the one who thought this AI experiment was crazy, but maybe you're letting some sort of bias close your mind to this possibility. Remember, you were the one who said that AI sometimes might open minds to ideas that no one ever considered?"

"Well, what should we do next?" Ned asked.

Avery sighed. "I don't know. I am suddenly remembering an article that I read that said AI can sometimes act like a 'crazy drunk friend.' Is that what's happening here? We're not drunk, but maybe this AI technology is?"

For the next two hours, the law clerks were busy sleuthing. In addition to AI, they did Google searches, went to public databases, and went to different "true crime" websites and blogs and podcasts. They typed in "Who is Misty Moses"—sometimes getting information and sometimes not. There were many people named "Misty Moses" all over the country—one could get phone and address information for many of them and family members and others with whom they might be living. One could get arrest records for some of them and lawsuit information. One of the law clerks even started typing messages to different true crime podcasters and bloggers, asking if they had ever explored this unsolved mystery and even the Misty Moses theory. Some of these podcasters and bloggers responded right away with enthusiasm for the subject—wanting to pursue the lead.

Avery wrapped it up around 1:30 a.m., offering her couches to anyone who was too tired to drive home. She said she was baffled and worried about what had just happened. Had they just opened Pandora's box?

"Judge, why are you so concerned? It's not like this is a real court case in front of us, where we're not allowed to go onto the internet and review 'extra-judicial information,' as you always say. We don't have anything to do with this case. None of us. We're just interested bystanders, I guess you could say. Trying to crack a cold case that no one is paying attention to anymore."

"I know. I just don't know where this Misty Moses theory came from. Maybe she is a totally innocent person who doesn't deserve anyone going down this trail. Maybe this is one of those infamous false outputs that the AI programs sometimes generate for no logical reason."

The law clerks looked at her with tired eyes.

Millicent spoke up. "Judge, you taught us better than maybe you think you did. We get what you're saying. Truly. We just have become fascinated by this unsolved mystery just like you have. We hate to see a life taken with no accountability. Gigi deserves better. Everyone deserves better."

"Yes, Gigi deserves better. I wholeheartedly agree with that. She deserves the dignity of bringing her killer to justice. But just remember, the whole situation deserves dignity. Suspects who are pulled out of left field—who might have nothing to do with the murder—deserve dignity. Good night."

Avery walked upstairs, and her dogs followed.

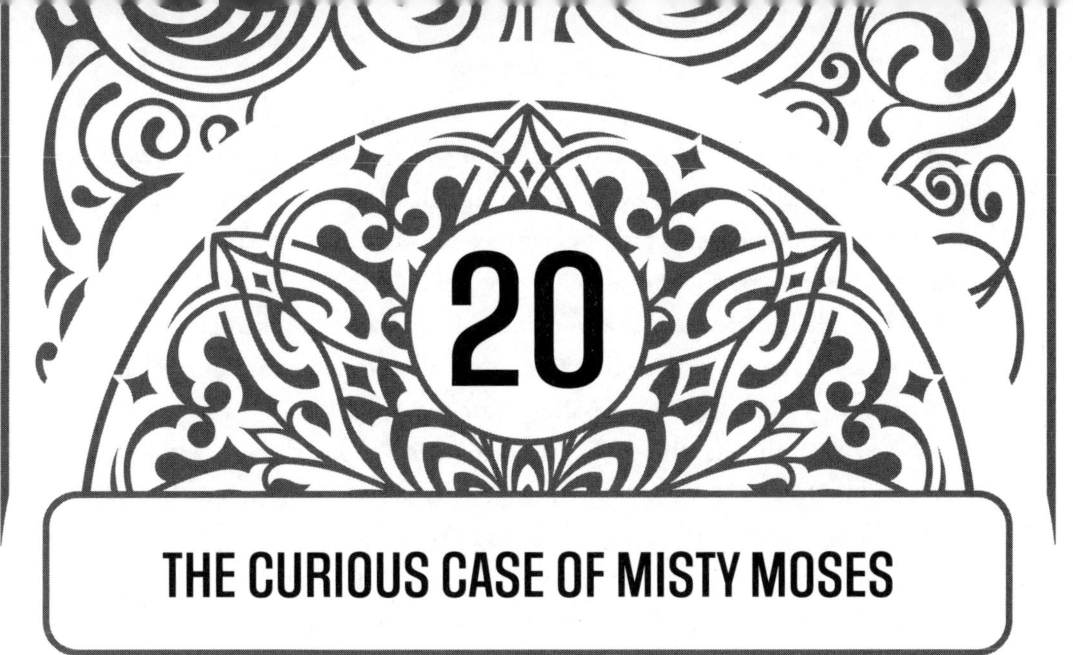

20

THE CURIOUS CASE OF MISTY MOSES

PRESENT DAY

In less than forty-eight hours, Misty Moses was virtually a household name—far and wide. Her possible connection to Gigi Mesero's murder "went viral," as the saying goes. Two of the most popular podcasters in the true crime world, Samantha Maben of the *Enigma* podcast and Harli Mace of the *Bloody Harli* blog and podcast, were hot on Misty's trail. They had broadcast to their legion of loyal followers that there was a new lead in the Genevieve Mesero unsolved murder case. How many followers did these podcasters have? It was published as being in the millions, although the genuine answer was uncertain—given Samantha's and Harli's regular use of internet-traffic-generating social media consultants, who had a knack for miraculously boosting their numbers. They each announced on their podcasts that they "had it on good information" that Misty Moses had apparently been a secret person of interest all along in this Texas cold case of the beautiful Latina heiress. The cops had apparently dropped the ball. Heads should roll for this incompetence. If anyone had any information about Misty Moses, they should contact them immediately—they were on the case. They and their team of investigators would follow up on all leads.

Soon, these true crime mavens had their social media consultants working more aggressively than ever, activating click farms in Bangladesh and the Philippines, who generated enormous amounts of new traffic to their blogs. These workers, clicking away on rows of mobile phones and laptops in remote cramped warehouses, earned one dollar per one thousand clicks. The workers earned bonus money for clicking on advertisements that appeared on Samantha's and Harli's websites. Samantha and Harli were getting thousands upon thousands of new hits and likes per day. Some were typing messages such as, "I know Misty. She told me she had killed people before," and "She bragged about having access to poison from her days working at a cat conservatory with her brother in Oklahoma." There were reports that Misty now lived back in Oklahoma at the cat conservatory. Other reports were that she was in a witness protection program and lived with a bunch of trans alpaca farmers in New Mexico. Still, others reported that she now worked in home healthcare or at a nursing home. And still, others reported that she now worked as a housekeeper for Flynn Fletcher and had killed Gigi at his request.

One morning, Homicide Detective Gil Gilmore walked into his office at the Dallas Police headquarters and flipped on his computer to check his emails first thing. He had three emails with "Misty Moses" in the subject line. He had yet another that stated: "Lead in Genevieve Mesero Cold Case—Misty Moses." He opened this latter one first. It was from his assistant chief, Alan Sarmiento, and stated: "Gil, I don't know who the hell Misty Moses is or why I am suddenly getting calls from media and amateur detectives about her being a person of interest in the Genevieve Mesero murder case. But I'm getting inundated. Where is this coming from, and why haven't you told me about this new lead? Please come see me immediately. I feel like one of us is about to get our ass chewed out over this. AS"

Gilmore began going through the other emails about Misty Moses. One was from a *Dallas Morning News* reporter. Another was from Frances Fletcher, Gigi's stepdaughter. Still another was from a retired detective, Ross Whitaker, who had worked on the Mesero case with Gilmore. All of these message-senders wanted to know where this new lead had suddenly come from and if Misty Moses had been a suspect all along. Why had her name been kept quiet until now?

Gilmore sighed in frustration. What the fuck?

He dialed Ross Whitaker first before he called his assistant chief. Gilmore had no memory whatsoever of Misty Moses.

What the hell was going on?

When Whitaker answered his phone, his first words were, "What the hell, Gil? Tell me about this new lead that everyone is buzzing about. How'd you get this new break in the Mesero case?"

Gil responded, "Ross, there is no new break in the Mesero case. I don't know where this is all coming from. This is hitting me from left field. Do you remember anyone named Misty Moses ever being mentioned?"

"Are you kidding me? You don't know who this is, either? Well, who does know if we don't know? This is nuts! But I tell you, you should do a Google search right now of Misty Moses. You're not going to believe what you see."

"Shit. This is insane. I'll get back to you, but Sarmiento wants to see me ASAP. I'm probably going to get fired over this." Gil hung up the phone and did a Google search, and there were dozens of hits regarding Misty Moses. News stories on supposed news sites that he had never heard of—amateur journalists, no doubt. Discussions on true crime sites. Special websites dedicated to Misty Moses with names like *Where Is Misty Moses?* and *Misty the Murderer*. A prevailing theory seemed to be that she worked as a home healthcare nurse now, under different aliases, and she robbed elderly people of their money and jewelry and then laced their medicine with strychnine, and no one ever suspected it was anything other than natural causes.

As Gilmore returned to his email box and further scrolled through his emails, he saw several messages requesting investigations into various deaths of elderly people at the Northgate Senior Living Center over the last two years. Relatives were thinking they were possible homicides. Apparently, Misty Moses had worked there until recently, and family members were now wondering if she had poisoned their loved ones.

Gilmore's phone rang. It was Assistant Chief Sarmiento. Gilmore answered, "I am on my way down to see you right now. I don't know anything about this Misty Moses insanity, but we'll get to the bottom of it."

21

THE OFFICIAL INVESTIGATION OF MISTY MOSES

PRESENT DAY

In the weeks ahead, the Dallas Police homicide division turned its attention back to the Genevieve Mesero cold case. How could they have neglected to investigate Misty Moses? Was this a terrible oversight on the part of the investigation team? They had talked quite extensively with Aldo Moses, and he had no hesitation in cooperating with officers. He took them to each camera at the Mystic Spires and gave them access to anything they wanted. He willingly answered questions. Officers followed up with him a few times. They even went inside his filthy trailer on occasion. There was no sign that anyone was living with him at the time of Gigi's death. They had no reason to ask him about his own family members or if he had any who visited him. While Misty Moses may have turned up at one time or another on a list of former Mystic Spires employees and may have been revealed as a person whose employment was terminated for cause, there was absolutely no reason to be very concerned about that. Employees came and went fairly frequently at the Mystic Spires. And, of course, there was a large group of suspects who had significant motive and likely opportunity. The prospect of this being a murder committed by a disgruntled former employee—one who had only worked there a short time—seemed inconceivable. Did the investigators drop the ball? Gil Gilmore was mortified. He had spent well over a thousand hours working on this case, chasing down every conceivable lead.

Gil Gilmore spent day and night the next few days going through boxes in the evidence room, looking for anything he missed. They had taken dozens of statements from different people with knowledge about Gigi's life. They had large amounts of forensic evidence. They had studied financial data about the Mesero business and Gigi's personal affairs. They had studied camera videos on nearby properties and license scans within a five-mile radius. They had studied social media accounts for every employee and all family and friends in the Mesero universe. Nothing had turned up about Misty. Misty had a couple of misdemeanor arrests in Oklahoma ten years ago. Nothing too serious. She hung out with some losers. But her social media presence was almost nonexistent. She had, indeed, worked at a senior living facility in Dallas in recent years. She appeared to be in Louisiana now doing home healthcare and cleaning services, interchangeably. Investigators would soon be visiting her there.

Gil Gilmore called Max Lassiter one Friday afternoon on a whim. It was two weeks after the Lassiters' AI law clerk party.

"Hey, buddy. How have you been?" Max said cheerfully when he answered the phone.

"Well, I've been better. I'm calling you about something on a long shot. I've had to revisit the Gigi Mesero murder investigation. I don't know if you are aware of this—it's been in the news some—not the mainstream news—but a new suspect has hit our radar screen, and I'm calling anyone and everyone who ever had anything to do with the investigation to see if anyone has ever heard this name. Misty Moses."

"Oh, shit. When did she become a suspect?"

"You know the name?"

"Well, yeah, sort of."

"What do you mean sort of?"

"If I tell you, you are going to think it's the craziest thing you ever heard. Please, just tell me, when did she become a suspect?"

"Well, just a few days ago. It wasn't anything on my end. It's not like we had any newly discovered evidence or happened on any evidence we'd previously ignored. We just started getting inundated by random calls and messages on our police hotline that she lived at the Mystic Spires in her brother's trailer at the time of the murder, and she had been a housekeeper there and had been fired a few days before. Allegedly, there are some folks who say she admitted killing Mesero and had access to poison and whatnot. This literally just came up days ago. Sarmiento is furious with me for failing to pursue this lead. We are having members of the public and media calling us idiots."

"Holy shit. I've got something to tell you. I don't know if this is coincidental timing or not. But my gut has me very worried that this is not a coincidence."

"Max, what are you saying? What do you know?"

"I hope you are sitting down. This is probably going to be the strangest thing you've heard all day. And if my hunch is right about how Misty Moses has now cropped up as a suspect, my wife is never going to stop saying 'I told you so' for the rest of my life."

"Max, what gives?"

"Tell you what. Let me run down to the station. I need to tell you about a mystery dinner party that we had here at the house a couple of weeks ago. I am very concerned that this Misty Moses theory is just social media gone wild."

"Well, I don't know what you mean by a mystery dinner party, but social media is definitely going wild over Misty Moses."

22

WHY MISTY?

PRESENT DAY

It was an overcast Sunday afternoon, and Max walked into Avery's home study. She was sitting in the dark in front of her laptop computer. Her favorite screensaver was turned on, which was a picture of the Guggenheim Museum in Bilbao, Spain.

"Avery, why are you sitting in the dark?"

"Oh, I don't know. It helps me clear my head sometimes. Remember when that NFL football player Aaron Rodgers famously went on his darkness retreat in an underground closet-like structure in some remote wooded area? Like for several days he sat in the dark in silence? Maybe I should do something like that sometime."

"No, you shouldn't. What's on your mind?"

"Max, why do you think that AI would come up with Misty Moses as an alternative theory as to who killed Gigi?"

"I should have known this is what you were stewing over. I don't know, Avery. It's like I've said. AI is not infallible. It's not something we can rely on with any certainty. It apparently puts data points together and comes up with something it thinks is logical based on those data points. God knows where it even got data points about Misty Moses."

"You used the word 'thinks.' AI comes up with something it 'thinks' is logical. AI can't think. It's not human."

"Well, true, sort of. It certainly can't feel like a human. But the platform was created by scientists trying to construct a neural network similar to human brains. So, it sort of is thinking. It compiles the data available to it and generates a possible result based on so-called algorithms, which are like formulas that are sort of 'if this, then that.'"

Avery stared. "I have been reading a lot about AI. Do you remember the movie called *The Imitation Game*? And the man that movie was based on—a guy named Alan Turing?"

"Uh, yeah. He figured out the Nazis' cryptography codes in World War Two. I don't know where this is going."

"Alan Turing is known for the Turing Test, and he was really an early pioneer of AI. The Turing Test was sort of a game where you put a computer in one room and a human in another room, and yet another human—the contestant—in the main room. The contestant would type questions out, and both the computer and the human in the other rooms would get those typed questions and type answers. Just typing. The game was to see if the human contestant could figure out which typed answers were from the human and which were from the computer. Many times, the human contestant could not tell which was the computer. In that situation, the computer was viewed as having passed the test."

"What do you mean? What test?"

"Well, it's the Turing Test. Alan Turing said that when we got to the point where a machine or computer could exhibit behavior that is equivalent to or indistinguishable from human behavior, that would be a significant step in the evolution of artificial intelligence."

"Okay. Well, that isn't necessarily the same thing as saying the computers can think, right? Is that where you're going with this?"

"Well, I guess that's debatable. The computer comes up with such convincing answers to questions that it fools the human contestant into thinking he is communicating with a human. Must be partly because the machine is coming up with better answers. Clever answers. Maybe the computer is processing information and thinking of a better answer than the human."

"Okay. I still don't know where you are going with this."

"I am worried. AI came up with an answer for who killed Gigi and the world who lives on the internet has decided AI knows best. Knows better than the police."

"Well, that's just idiots on the internet. Avery, an AI-generated lead would never create probable cause to obtain a warrant. Any law enforcement officer would only use it as a theory—maybe as a starting point—to explore something that maybe hadn't been explored."

"Well, I hope the world never gets to the point where we all think what AI generates is enough to create probable cause. What do you think the data points might have been to cause Misty Moses to be spat out as a possible suspect?"

"Well, I'm just speculating. But maybe there was a public record somewhere of her being terminated after working at the Mystic Spires—say, an unemployment compensation benefit request through the State of Texas. Or an EEOC complaint. Experience shows that sometimes disgruntled employees act out in bad ways against former employers. So, if AI had that kind of data, maybe it made a deduction from it. And maybe Misty had used her brother's address at the Mystic Spires and that is showing up in people-finder sites. She also had a criminal record—albeit an old misdemeanor—but still publicly available. She had a thug boyfriend—old man Worm. Who knows what else is out there in a public database or social media regarding him? Maybe she had an old Facebook or Instagram account where she posted things about the Mesero murder. It's circumstantial evidence—I guess you'd say compiled from the internet, maybe accessed by the AI platform."

"Well, would the police have interviewed her based on any of this data?"

"Maybe. I truly don't know if anyone did. Remember, it was not my case."

"Where do you think she is now?"

"Probably in hiding if she knows what's going on. Wouldn't you be if Samantha Maben and Bloody Harli and all the other true crime conspiracy theorists were obsessed with you?"

"I don't know. Maybe I'd want to clear my name."

23

A CASE OF MISTAKEN IDENTITY?

PRESENT DAY

Misty Moses quietly sat on her mother's screened-in back porch overlooking the secluded cove on Lake of the Ozarks where her mother's small, framed cottage was located. Her German shepherd Brutus snored at her feet. She smoked a cigarette and listened to the sounds of nature at sundown, interrupted by the occasional buzz of a speedboat or bass boat zipping through the waterway at the end of the cove. Mostly retirees lived around here, enjoying their golden years at the huge, winding, tree-lined lake. They called this lake the "Magic Dragon" because of its twisting, zigzagging shoreline. Misty's eighty-seven-year-old mother, Maureen Moses, had Alzheimer's and various other health ailments. Misty spent every day, almost all day, caring for her mother. It was tough. But there was no one else to do it. And she wanted to do it. Misty obtained government assistance for doing it, as she had been designated as a home healthcare aide.

Misty heard the phone inside ringing. It was a landline. It was the only reliable phone out here. Misty's mother had no internet service, and cell phone reception was spotty. Misty decided to ignore it. It was probably bill collectors. But it kept ringing and ringing. It would stop for a couple of minutes, then start again. She eventually worried it would wake up her mother. She went inside and picked up the phone in the kitchen.

"Hello? Who is this, and why do you keep calling?"

"Is this Misty Moses?"

"Who wants to know?"

"I'm trying to reach Misty Moses. I have something important I want to discuss with her."

"Unless I have won the Publishers Clearing House prize, I don't care what you have to say."

There was silence for a few moments. "I'd like to talk to you, Misty. This is Harli Mace. Have you heard of me?"

"No. Should I have heard of you?"

"I'd like to talk to you about Gigi Mesero. Would you be willing to talk to me?"

"Who the hell is Gigi Mesero?"

"You don't remember Gigi Mesero?"

Misty hung up the phone and went back out to the porch.

Harli Mace hung up her own phone and smiled at her assistant. "We've got her. I know that was her. Let's send a crew out. It looks like her address is in the middle of nowhere, but we'll find it."

The following afternoon, Harli Mace, three assistants, and a camera crew of two more people showed up in a souped-up van at the tiny cottage at the end of a dirt road on a cove of Sunrise Beach at Lake of the Ozarks. There was no mailbox and no identifying information to indicate it was Maureen Moses's residence. There was no car or other sign of human life, but a dog could be heard barking inside. Harli told the cameramen to start their cameras rolling. She was going to knock on the door, which still had a Christmas wreath hanging on it, although it was many weeks past the holiday. Harli wanted to live-stream her intended encounter with Misty Moses, although the reception was very spotty. They had brought along plenty of high-tech equipment, so hopefully, her plan would work. When the cameramen gave Harli the thumbs-up, she loudly knocked on the door several times. Brutus the German shepherd began barking more loudly and his clawed feet could be heard scratching on the inside of the door.

The only sound from indoors remained that of Brutus. Harli kept knocking and started calling out, "Misty Moses, are you in there? I'd like to talk to you."

Misty heard them all right. She had just finished bathing her mother and putting her down for a nap. She could not imagine who was outside. No one ever came out this way. Something bad must have happened.

Misty opened the door after about five minutes. There were camera lights, and Harli Mace was shoving a microphone in her face.

"What the hell is this? Who are you people?" Misty screamed, pushing Brutus back inside and closing the door behind her.

"We'd like to talk to Misty Moses," Harli said.

"I am Misty Moses. What do you want?"

Harli hesitated. She looked at her phone and then at her assistants.

"But you're biracial. And skinny."

"Last I checked, neither one of those things was a crime," Misty replied.

Harli looked confused. Then she spoke up to her assistants. "Everything you've pulled up shows that Misty Moses is a redheaded, fair-skinned Caucasian. Blue eyes. Very heavy build. No plastic surgeon in the world could pull this off." Harli was pointing to a Misty who was brown-eyed, brown-skinned, with long dark braids. She probably weighed a hundred twenty pounds.

"You've got ten seconds to tell me what the hell this is all about. After that, I'm calling the cops. Rest assured, we do have 911 out here, even though it sometimes takes them a bit to get here. I've got Brutus to take care of business if the cops take too long."

Harli was now furious. She turned to her assistants. "You idiots! You sent us to the wrong Misty Moses. You said you were positive this was the right one. We drove out to BFE for nothing. Jesus Christ! I am surrounded by incompetence!"

As Harli angrily turned to head back into their van, a barefoot Maureen Moses stepped out of the front door in a pink nightgown with a 12-gauge shotgun in her hands. "Who are you people? What's going on? Leave us alone! Stand back or I'll shoot every last one of you!"

Misty screamed in horror. "Mother, please go into the house. It's okay."

Maureen Moses then pulled the trigger on the shotgun three times. The blasts were wide. Misty was hit. Both Harli Mace and one cameraman were hit. Harli's wounds were not lethal. Misty and the cameraman died.

24

OBITUARY PIRATES

PRESENT DAY

"Hi, Mom. You're not going to believe what I just found when researching Gigi."

Julia Lassiter was typing rapidly on her laptop at the kitchen table, giving occasional attention to her beeping iPhone.

It was 7 p.m., and Avery had just dragged in from work. Avery placed her own laptop on the kitchen table near Julia's. The Lassiters' kitchen table was everyone's temporary workstation when meals weren't being served. Jake and Finley were twirling and panting at Avery's feet because they knew that her arrival home meant they would soon be fed dinner.

Avery went to the refrigerator to get the dogs' food and began dishing it into their bowls. She noticed with relief that Max had already started dinner from the smell of garlic and basil wafting from the oven.

"Julia, what do you mean you're researching Gigi? Number one, have you already finished your homework? And number two, assuming you have, why is this the way you choose to spend your free time?"

"Why can't I research Gigi like the rest of the world, Mom?"

"Good lord, Julia! Do you really think it has come to that? You think the whole world is paying attention to this hype over Gigi?"

"Uh, yeah. Don't you pay attention to the internet, Mom?"

"Well, I pay enough attention to have grave concerns about the future of humanity and its values. But then I remember that there's a lot of smoke and mirrors on the internet, so what I'm seeing might not be entirely reflective of what is really going on with society."

Julia looked at her mother with a skeptical face.

Wonder where Julia got her skepticism . . .

Avery snickered out loud a bit, realizing that this might be the one and only trait that her daughter shared with her mom. Skepticism about everything. Other than that, she was the female version of her father. Actually, her father was a skeptic, too.

"Mom, are you about to give your weekly speech about how the internet is the harbinger of society's collapse?"

"Maybe. But back to what you said, Julia, that I wasn't going to believe what you found about Gigi. What did you mean?"

"Well, there are these videos on YouTube where these men just sit in a chair—it's usually men, not women—and they read obituaries in a creepy, monotone voice. Almost like they are robots. And I stumbled across a few of them reading Gigi's obituary. It's morbid and weird! There are like a dozen of them."

"You have got to be kidding me," Avery said with a concerned look on her face. She put the dog food back in the refrigerator and got two carrots out to give the dogs for dessert.

"Show me what you're talking about, Julia."

Avery walked up behind Julia and peeked over her shoulder at her laptop.

Julia began explaining as she typed. "Okay, so there are actually websites and also YouTube videos. The websites aren't all that creepy. They just seem to be full of normal obituaries, maybe harvested from a funeral home website or newspapers. And they advertise a lot of things relating to death, like life insurance and funeral homes and florists and cards. I guess the websites aren't that weird. But let me show you the YouTube videos."

Julia clicked on the first of a huge number of disturbing videos, to say the least. The first one showed a middle-aged white man sitting in a chair in what looked like a living room, speaking emotionlessly directly into the camera.

He appeared to be reading Gigi's obituary from somewhere like Legacy.com. The video was low quality. It showed it had hundreds of thousands of views. There was an advertisement for retinol face cream next to it that one could click on, as well as other ads for myriad products.

"Click on some of the others, Julia."

One by one, Julia clicked on the various YouTube videos that had popped up after she searched "Gigi Mesero death." The videos were all similar. Some had slideshows of pictures of Gigi, likely pulled from social media or other public sources, playing intermittently next to the speaker. Sometimes, they were dark and shadowy, and sometimes there were candles and flowers but never any warmth or emotion. Sometimes, there were details about the brutality of her death—in a different, more morbid style than a simple obituary. The speakers were always robotic.

"This is absolutely macabre. Horrible!"

Max burst into the kitchen and peeked inside the oven. "Hey, Avery. I didn't hear you come home. My lasagna still needs another fifteen minutes."

Avery looked up. "Smells yummy. But will you come over here and look at these crazy YouTube videos Julia just discovered? We are both horrified!"

"What now? Some stupid new stunt kids are trying? Please tell me kids aren't eating something like Tide Pods again."

"Uh, no. Please just come look. It's about Gigi."

"Oh, good grief! Do you two ever give it a rest? Y'all have got to stop obsessing over Gigi."

"Max, we're not obsessing."

"I think you are."

"Just come look, please."

Max approached the kitchen table with an annoyed expression.

Julia played one of the videos. This one had Rachmaninov piano music playing softly in the background while the robotic man casually recited facts about Gigi's life and death. The dramatic music accompaniment made this video even creepier than the other videos she had played so far for Avery.

Max shrugged his shoulders. "Oh, that's just an obituary pirate. Yeah, that's been a thing for a while. It's messed up. You hopefully realize that they aren't just doing YouTube videos about Gigi's death. You can find thousands of those amateur videos. It's like a cottage industry."

"You know about these? It's a thing?"

"Yes, Avery. Any cop will tell you that they regularly follow obituaries. Cops like to keep apprised as to whether any of the criminals they're looking for end up dying. Makes life easier. Investigation closed."

Avery looked at Max with a furrowed brow. "Really? That sounds kind of harsh."

"Well, it's true. Anyway, videos like that have been out there for a few years now. It's internet entrepreneurs profiteering off people's deaths by making low-budget videos reading or summarizing death notices or, in a high-profile situation like Gigi's, maybe they pull from multiple data sources and essentially just republish. They are geeks with skills in search engine optimization, so they can pull lots of internet traffic to their sites and then they can use that traffic to charge money to people who want to place ads on their websites next to their videos."

Avery sighed. "Okay. So, basically, these people are monetizing people's deaths. Making money off the clicks they get."

"Yep. Are you really surprised? In *our* jobs, why should we ever be surprised?"

"It's hard to believe they could make much money off this, but maybe they can. Some of these videos show several thousand views. A few look like they have over a million. Some of the ones about Gigi are approaching eight hundred thousand views."

"Maybe they can thank Bloody Harli Mace for all those hits on the Gigi videos. Or maybe it should just be chalked up to human nature. People are fascinated by death."

"This almost feels like it shouldn't be legal. But I guess it's free speech. I don't know. Maybe it could be copyright infringement in certain circumstances. But good luck catching or stopping these 'internet entrepreneurs,' as you call them. Immoral scumbags, if you ask me."

"Yeah. Being immoral or distasteful isn't a crime or grounds for a lawsuit. At least not in this country yet."

Avery turned back to Julia. "Let's clear off our stuff, sweetie, and set the table for dinner. I can't stand looking at these videos anymore. Let's pretend we never saw them."

"Don't you want to hear about another website I discovered today, Mom?" Julia pressed. "There's a ghost hunter's website that describes how the Mystic Spires Hotel was well known to be haunted. Windows opened and closed all the time. Women's voices were heard by guests when no one else was around. Shadowy figures moving around. Cold spots. Objects moving. And a woman walking around in a light-colored dress that looked just like the Lioness, Gigi's mother who was killed in a plane crash. Maybe there's a supernatural explanation for Gigi's death."

Avery shook her head, sighed, and walked to the wine fridge.

"Mom, don't act like it's not possible!"

"Julia, every old hotel in the country is rumored to be haunted. It's a universal thing. Please. Use your brain."

"Think about how many people died there. Think about how many fires there were. It's like the hotel was alive. Until it wasn't."

25

GIGI MESERO'S BANKRUPTCY CASE FILE

Gigi Mesero filed a personal bankruptcy case a few years before her death. Police had not paid much attention to this fact. Debt is a fact of life in the modern world. It is not uncommon for people to partake of the cleansing bath of bankruptcy. Businesses do it, and people do it. Celebrities do it. Athletes do it. A past governor of Texas once famously did it. Even former U.S. presidents have done it. Some regard it as a business strategy. In many ways, it is. Sometimes it heals and renews and saves. Sometimes it only prolongs a collapse.

The thing about bankruptcy is that your life becomes an open book. "Open kimono" is the metaphor used. You file paperwork (electronically on the court's website) listing your address and phone number and all of your assets and liabilities. The names and addresses of all of your creditors are listed. Your salary and expenses are listed. Transfers of assets and gifts must be disclosed. All of this information is publicly available. You're a little bit like a fish in a glass aquarium. It's the price you pay for the fresh start. Creditors usually don't like it much. Not only are they mad about unpaid debts owed to them, but some would rather the world not see that they dealt with the bankrupt person. Maybe they do not want people to know about a foolish business decision. Maybe they simply don't want their name and address in the public domain. But some statutes and rules require open access to this information to the public. It is believed that transparency is necessary for the integrity of the system.

The tragic event at Lake of the Ozarks involving Harli Mace, her cameraman, and the "wrong" Misty Moses—who never knew Gigi Mesero—did not slow down the fervor of the true crime enthusiasts. They were back to their sleuthing in a few short days. This time, someone had the idea of digging into the publicly available bankruptcy files of Gigi Mesero. Some angry creditor, perhaps, had a beef with Gigi that the police ignored. This theory was fueled when someone published a transcript he had found of Gigi's testimony at a hearing. At the beginning of her testimony, a lawyer asked Gigi the usual questions that are asked of any witness, about whether she was under the influence of any substance or there was anything else that might impair her testimony. Gigi replied, "I took NyQuil last night, which is my usual habit, but I'm pretty sure it's worn off by now." This set off a firestorm of true crime podcasting chatter, with some speculating that every creditor in Gigi's case knew about her NyQuil habit and should be evaluated as a possible suspect.

The bankruptcy files were actually quite juicy, even to the uninitiated. There were schedules of assets describing the contents of the Mystic Spires penthouse that Gigi called home. There was valuable artwork and antiques. Gigi had expensive jewelry, including a 6.32 carat rare pink diamond that her father had given to her mother for her thirtieth birthday, and another magnificent tanzanite-and-platinum Tiffany Victoria ring that her sister had given her. She had Chanel purses, Hermès scarves, Jimmy Choo shoes, every color of Miron Crosby women's cowboy boots ever made, Gucci anything, and Prada everything. She had Tiffany bone china and lead crystal glasses. She owned an Aston Martin car. She had a vacation home in the Canary Islands.

And Gigi had lots of debt, of course. In addition to signing personal guarantees on various business loans for Belleza Mistica, LLC, she had hundreds of thousands of dollars of credit card debt and IRS tax debt. It was hard to comprehend how things had gotten so out of hand.

The true crime sleuths shared these juicy nuggets they found and compared theories. Many speculated that the bankruptcy case was the treasure trove of information that the cops had not explored. Perhaps some banker at a bank that loaned money to Gigi got fired when she filed for bankruptcy and caused the bank huge losses. The banks and their loan officers were all there in print—in the publicly available file—if people wanted to research each and every one of them. What about the Aston Martin dealership? Could someone over there have gotten his head handed to him when Gigi drove the car that he sold her off the lot, and then she promptly defaulted on the car loan? Maybe she had been having an affair with one of these lenders or other creditors and their wives found out? Gigi's list of creditors showed some medical debts including one to an ob-gyn. Maybe Gigi was pregnant!

Avery learned about this sleuthing in the most unpleasant way. One Monday morning, a motion to seal the Gigi Mesero bankruptcy file was on her desk. It had been filed by an interior designer who had been a creditor in Gigi's case because of some unpaid bills for redecorating her penthouse. It seems that the interior decorator had been through a terrible divorce and obtained a temporary restraining order against her ex-husband, who had been stalking her. Her address and all her private information were unlisted, and she had gone to great pains to keep herself and her home under the radar. The true crime sleuths had published on websites the list of creditors in Gigi's bankruptcy case, and this included the interior designer's address and phone number and the amount of money she was owed by Gigi. The sleuths were asking people if they knew anyone on this list. The interior designer's ex-husband saw this information and had recently come to her house and brutally attacked her. She had now hired a lawyer to attempt to seal her personal information that was identifiable in the bankruptcy case—although the damage had pretty much been done at this point.

26

IN THE FUTURE, THERE WILL BE NO CRIME?

PRESENT DAY

"Hey, Max, do you remember that Philip K. Dick sci-fi novel where he said in the future there will be no crime?"

Max looked up from his phone at Avery and shook his head no.

"It was a book about these bots or mutant beings of some sort that would dream about and predict a crime before it happened, and then law enforcement would be alerted when these bots had their visions about a future crime, and then this 'pre-crime special task force' of cops would go arrest someone before they committed the crime. For a pre-crime." Avery looked at Max as he gave her a side glance that signaled, *Wonder where she's going with this . . .*

"Well, actually, I remember a Tom Cruise movie about that kind of thing called *Minority Report.* But the crime-predictors were called 'pre-cogs,' not bots. They were mutant people that were children of drug addicts, who were plugged into this big machine."

"Yeah, that's it! That movie was made based on the Philip K. Dick book. He was an amazing sci-fi writer. You remembered the details better than me."

"And?"

"Did you ever feel that way when you were a cop? I mean, not necessarily that there would be no crime in the future. But that no one would ever get away with a crime in the future. I remember you told me that during your last couple of years on the force you could literally solve tons of crimes just sitting at your desk. Faster than ever before, by just looking at Ring doorbell cameras, toll road cameras, business security cameras, and license plate readers. Even drone footage. Oh, and those gunshot detection sensors."

"And don't forget people's social media posts. Amazing how criminals brag on their social media posts about the scores they just made or the licks they just hit."

Avery looked at Max strangely, realizing that she was constantly learning new slang that criminals use.

"Well, how did you feel about all that?" Avery said.

"What do you mean how did I feel about all that? I felt great when I solved a crime. Technology can be a beautiful thing."

Avery rolled her eyes. "Well, did you ever feel like you were taking an easy, lazy way out? Maybe taking shortcuts?"

"Why would I feel that way? I've told you before that technology is just a starting place. It can present data to you that you wouldn't otherwise come across, and help you make sense of the data. But we would never try to get warrants for probable cause based solely on anything AI produced. Those facial recognition systems, in particular, can be prone to errors. But sometimes they are great. You just have to be careful. Be smart about it."

"Well, what about when you spy on someone's social media posts? I assume that's only when it's publicly available, not private? Like, not if the user marked it private?"

"Not necessarily. I mean, if I send some suspect a 'friend request' using a pseudonym, and the suspect is stupid enough to accept it, and then I see his private social media posts, and he has pictures of himself standing next to a pile of cash or a warehouse of stolen stuff, then hell yeah, I'm going to take advantage of that situation and try to solve a crime. I probably could get a warrant based off that. But it's not like I'm going to accept anything I see on social media or the internet generally as one hundred percent true or reliable. The guy posting pictures could be a great photoshopper and makes shit up to impress his girlfriend."

"Ugh. The thought of some woman being impressed by that."

"You crack me up. You have no idea how some people live."

"Uh, I see a pretty large share of humanity in my job, too, Max."

"It's a matter of degree, Avery. After you've had to spend a day searching through the city dump for evidence or had to clean up vomit and urine from the back of your squad car after a twelve-hour shift, come talk to me more about experiencing humanity, honey."

"Max! You are being gross now."

"Anyway, the whole *Minority Report* plot was entirely different, Avery. It was about predictive policing. Using AI in conjunction with those pre-cogs to predict and prevent crime. That's a whole different subject. Much more controversial, I'd say. Predictive AI is about using past information or community data regarding crime trends to make predictions and allocate resources to areas based on algorithms. This is fraught with risks. It gets into the whole profiling thing. What I used occasionally was *assistive* AI, not *predictive* AI. Anyway, where is this conversation going? Is this going to be another one of your conversations about how AI is the harbinger of the collapse of society? And bemoaning that the whole internet is going crazy, investigating Gigi Mesero's murder?"

"I don't know. Maybe. Yes. It's just all so mind-boggling to me. I mean, it's wonderful that there's this vast amount of technology now that can help cops solve crimes. And I know you used to say that federal and local law enforcement agencies talk to one another more than ever before, sharing their accumulated data and whatnot. And that watching out for chatter on the internet often helps law enforcement. I'm just so afraid where this all could go. Could we eventually abdicate all of our thinking to these machines? What about human instincts and hunches and reading a person's body language? Looking into their eyes? What about the burden of proof? A machine cannot understand these nuances—they cannot distinguish things like preponderance of the evidence versus clear and convincing evidence versus beyond a reasonable doubt. A machine cannot differentiate among concepts like "possible," and "plausible," and "probable." These are concepts that matter in the law. It requires deep thinking. We still have the best justice system that humans have ever conceived—even if it's flawed and we occasionally can't solve a murder case like poor Gigi's. But we can't just delegate thinking and analysis to machines. And we sure can't delegate crime-solving to a horde of amateur detectives chatting with each other in cyberspace."

"I really don't think we are in danger of that happening, Avery."

"It's happening as we speak, Max. Right now. People in their mother's basements are chatting in cyberspace, trying to solve Gigi's death. They have no idea what the cops have and have not investigated. They have no idea what they are doing. They have no respect for the dignity of the process and people's rights. These people think they know what they are doing and are smarter than law enforcement and prosecutors. But they aren't, and they also aren't guided by rules, procedures, or the Constitution, for that matter. There's a reason we have all these things."

Max started putting leashes on Jake and Finley. It was starting to seem like a good time to walk the dogs. They began yapping with excitement.

"And what about this new reality of cameras everywhere, Max? I mean, on the one hand, it's great, I suppose, if it's a great crime-solving tool or even a deterrent. But are we becoming a police state? Is Big Brother always watching us? You even told me that Walmart has the best security system imaginable. Cameras and buying histories for people. Soon, I guess that will be everywhere."

"Avery, calm down. I don't know about Big Brother, but our Alexa is listening. She might think you are crazy and report you to the authorities."

"Oh, stop making fun of me. This is a big deal. If people like us, who are part of the system, don't think through this and talk about these things, then who will?"

"Sweetheart, I am no longer part of the system. I am retired."

"Stop bragging."

Max handed Avery Jake's leash. "Come on. The dogs are getting impatient."

Avery took Jake's leash. "Max, you sometimes hear people worrying about what will happen if AI gets sentient. First, they can think and then they might perceive or be able to feel things. I think we are worried about the wrong thing. I am worried about people no longer thinking or feeling. They just let AI sort it all out."

"Avery, Jake and Finley don't want to hear anymore of this. Not tonight."

27

A CHANCE ENCOUNTER IN SHREVEPORT

PRESENT DAY

Flynn Fletcher had seen better days. After his divorce from Gigi and eventual acquittal on his criminal bribery and corruption charges, he floundered for a bit. He knew he needed to get out of Texas. He considered returning to New Jersey for a while. But he had burned a few too many bridges there and had no desire to resurrect his career as the Flamethrower, practicing personal injury law. Eventually, his connections in the casino industry proved handy. He formed a janitorial business that obtained contracts with several of the casino properties in Louisiana. It was a pretty lucrative gig. He eventually had a rather large workforce and recruited some acquaintances from his past to help run the business. One of those acquaintances from his past was Aldo Moses—who was always good about doing anything Flynn asked of him during the brief time Flynn lived at the Mystic Spires. And Aldo, in turn, reached out to his sister, Misty, to help with the business. By this time, Misty was known as Misty Darnell. She had, two years ago, married a New Mexico alpaca farmer and took and kept his surname, even though the marriage had been short-lived.

Misty's decision to take the alpaca farmer's surname proved to be fortuitous. When the internet exploded with the Where's Misty Moses? circus,

Misty Darnell was completely oblivious to it, and nobody had zeroed in on her. She worked long hours for decent pay. She kept a low profile. She had no social media presence and spent no time on the internet. Her red hair was now gray, and her blue eyes were tired and covered with thick glasses. She was heavier than ever and walked with a limp. She lived in a trailer park on the outskirts of Shreveport. She minded her own business. She smoked a little weed now and then but mostly stayed on the straight and narrow. She had an understanding of sorts with her ultimate boss, Flynn Fletcher. Keep your head down and do your job. Don't talk to strangers. Don't talk to cops. Put a "Back the Blue" sticker on your old Toyota, and the cops will never bother you. And, you scratch my back, and I'll scratch yours. You don't know nothin' about nothin'. That was mostly true, but not entirely.

One rainy September morning, Misty arrived at work and several local police officers were standing around the entrance of the janitorial business. A nearby business had been robbed overnight, and the cops were wondering if anyone on the overnight cleaning crews, coming and going, might have seen anything. Apparently, no one at the janitorial business had witnessed anything. One of the cops, a young Officer Dupree, noticed the name badge on Misty's uniform as she walked up to the entrance of the business. It simply said, "Misty." Officer Dupree had, at one time, lived in Dallas and had moved to Shreveport a couple of years earlier to be closer to family. Officer Dupree had already recognized the name of the business owner that he had earlier interviewed, Flynn Fletcher, as the ex-husband and suspect at one time in the infamous Dallas murder of Genevieve Mesero. He also had kept up with the recent internet buzz about Misty Moses. What were the odds? Could this be her?

Officer Dupree spoke up. "Hello, ma'am. Misty."

Misty realized that the officer had glanced down at her name badge. She wondered if he could smell marijuana on her.

"Hello, officer. What's going on here?"

"There was a burglary over at the auto supply shop overnight. We're just trying to determine if anyone saw anything."

"Oh, I don't know nothin'. I got off at five last night. I didn't see nothin'. I can't help you none."

"Okay. I'll give you my card in case you see or hear anything. Hope you'll call if you do."

Misty cautiously took his card.

"You know, you look sort of familiar to me. Have I met you before, ma'am?"

"I don't think so. I pretty much keep to myself. Don't get in no trouble."

"Oh, I didn't mean to imply that. You just have one of those familiar faces maybe. Wondered if you ever lived in Dallas? I used to live there and thought I may have known you there."

Misty's pale, freckled skin turned even paler. "I've got to go, officer. I've got properties to clean."

Misty scurried inside the janitorial offices in silence, looking rather nervous.

Officer Dupree looked at his colleague. "What are the odds?"

The colleague looked bewildered and shrugged.

"Have you been following any of that craziness about the Gigi Mesero unsolved murder case that happened in Dallas several years ago?"

"Nope."

"Hmmm. Well, I guess with my prior connection to Dallas, I've sort of paid more attention to it than I might have otherwise. I mean, I never worked on the case, but I was a rookie cop in Dallas when a murder of a wealthy, beautiful woman named Gigi Mesero occurred. People were so upset that an arrest was never made. Drove the police department nuts. Apparently, there are some new leads involving someone named Misty Moses. At least that's what I have been reading."

"You think that cleaning lady was her? The Misty they're suspecting now?"

"I don't know. The pictures that have been on the internet sort of look like a younger version of that cleaning lady. Maybe I'll call one of my former buddies on the force. Just in case."

Several hours later, Officer Dupree picked up the phone and texted one of his former colleagues at the Dallas Police Department.

—Hey, how've u been?

—Hey. Good to hear from you. I've been okay. Working third watch and weekends. Getting pretty tired of it. They're going to change our shifts up next week. Hoping to get a detective spot soon. How's Shreveport?

—It's good. Slower pace, for sure. Hey, do you know anything about this reopening of the Gigi Mesero case and the suspect, Misty Moses? Is all that true? Keep reading about it on the internet.

—Not sure. It's pretty hush-hush. Why?

—I think I may've seen Misty Moses today. Not sure. But she looks like an older version of the woman they're showing on the internet.

—Hmm. Let me check around and see who's working on this. I think it's Gil Gilmore. Remember him?

—Sure do. Good guy.

28

MYSTIC VAL, THE SOCIAL MEDIA INFLUENCER

PRESENT DAY

Valentina Mesero became quite the social media influencer in the years after the Mystic Spires burned to the ground (for the last time) and after she sold the remainder of the Belleza Mistica hotel empire to a private equity fund. She used the moniker "Mystic Val" for her influencer persona. She had five million followers, according to her Instagram account. Of course, who knows how many of those were real human followers versus bots or fakes generated by a click farm—courtesy of her social media consultant. In any event, Mystic Val got lots of advertising revenue from her perceived large, loyal following. Cosmetics, hair products, weight loss supplements, yoga clothing, shoes, jewelry lines—you name it, the companies targeting young to middle-aged females all loved to get Mystic Val to endorse their products. Every day of her life was documented for the world to see. It was every minute, some days. First thing in the morning, would she have a matcha tea or a protein shake? What vitamin supplements was she using today? How did she sleep? Not great—her cat, Madame Suki, slept on her head half the night—at which point she'd post a picture of her beloved feline, perhaps dressed up in a tutu. Would she go on a run this morning or ride her Peloton? She would have lunch later with her best friend from college, who was in town—what should she wear to lunch? She would lay out three possible outfits for people to rate. And where should they go to lunch? One of Tim Love's new restaurants maybe? Or maybe they should just go to some swanky bar and drink martinis and do caviar bumps all afternoon. Lol. What does everyone think? Then later there would be selfies posted with the friend, some with pouty duck lips and some others with big toothy smiles. There would be pictures of the food and drinks. Then pictures of them hugging goodbye with a note that they had planned a trip to Paris for Fashion Week later in the year. Then later, there would probably be some comments about some great new eye makeup remover she was going to try before going to bed tonight. It was vegan, had not been tested on animals, and was made in Switzerland by a company that leaves no carbon footprint. And, also, she would post that she was thinking about doing a colon cleanse tomorrow, although the Ozempic she was taking had caused her to lose so much weight that maybe she didn't need to after all. But she had to get into her bikini next week for the party at the Hamptons she was attending with her new boyfriend. LOL. Lots of "LOLs." And the next morning it would start all over.

Shortly after the internet exploded with Misty Moses theories, Mystic Val's postings took a busy but somber turn. "For those of you who don't know or don't remember, Gigi Mesero was my sister. My only sibling. This new theory about Misty Moses has me in anguish. I'm in absolute emotional turmoil. It's forcing me to relive one of the worst nights of my life!"

The reactions were prolific.

OMG, Val. We love you. We are with you.

Stay strong!

RIP Gigi.

You'll see her again in heaven.

F+k Misty Moses! You should hunt Misty Moses down and make her pay!*

This last message was repeated at different times with slightly different words.

Val, if I were you, I'd pay a private investigator to track Misty down and make her pay! You don't deserve to suffer this way! Your sister's killer needs to face justice!

Eventually, Val took a poll of her followers: "Who thinks I should track down Misty Moses?" The thumbs-up emojis were overwhelming.

"Hey, Mom." Julia walked into the kitchen as Avery was staring into their refrigerator, examining its dwindling contents for dinner ideas. "Guess what? Mystic Val is jumping on the Misty Moses bandwagon."

"What? Mystic Val? Who is that?" Avery knew she would regret asking.

"Valentina Mesero, Mom! Remember, we saw her at the Prague airport last Christmas. I told you that she was a social influencer now." Julia started to hand her phone to her mother to take a peek at Mystic Val's latest Instagram posts.

"Good lord, Julia. I've asked you not to waste your time and brain cells on these people. These influencers are not serious people. They are smoke and mirrors. Images that they want to project. One day, post-apocalypse, social scientists will write that the end of civilization began when people with no talent or skills started becoming millionaires for doing nothing. Nothing of value. Some of them are probably not even real people. Maybe AI generated. They're either mostly fake or totally fake."

"But Mom, we know Valentina is real. We saw her in Valencia and then again in Prague."

"Well, we think it was her in Prague. We didn't know for sure. I still wonder if it was her and if she really dates a drug cartel guy named El Gusano."

"Nope. She now dates a professional baseball player. A New York Yankee."

"Eww. That's even worse than a drug cartel member!"

"Mom!"

"I'm just kidding, of course. Wonder how she met him?"

"She lives in New York now. She posts pictures of her apartment and its views overlooking Central Park all the time. She lives at the Dakota. She brags all the time about how she miraculously was able to get an apartment there. Apparently, it's impossible."

"Julia, how do you know what New York properties are impossible to get in? Really. You're a teenager."

"Mom, have you heard of Google?"

"Of course. The oracle of truth. The only source of information that we should ever consult. But tell me about Valentina getting on the Misty Moses bandwagon. What exactly did you mean by that?"

"She's been chatting on her Instagram about all the Misty Moses hype and how this is all making her relive the worst day of her life. And all of her followers are encouraging her to hire a private investigator and track down and confront Misty Moses, and she's thinking about doing it."

"Fantastic. Let's live-steam another tragedy like the Harli Mace debacle. The world has gone crazy, I tell you. Do we need any more examples?"

Julia looked at her mother in silence. "Mom, I'm not the only one in this family who follows Valentina. Aunt Suzanne does, too. And Kat."

"Are you kidding me?"

Julia shook her head. "We chat about her a lot. And I don't think it's fair to say she's not a serious person. She graduated from your alma mater!"

Avery rolled her eyes. "Well, she's not an alumna who's using her education and personal resources to make the world a better place or solve problems. That's what I mean by not a serious person."

Julia looked in silence. The dogs burst through the doggie door wagging their tails. "They're hungry, Mom. So am I. What's for dinner?"

"What's Mystic Val having? Maybe we should have what she's having."

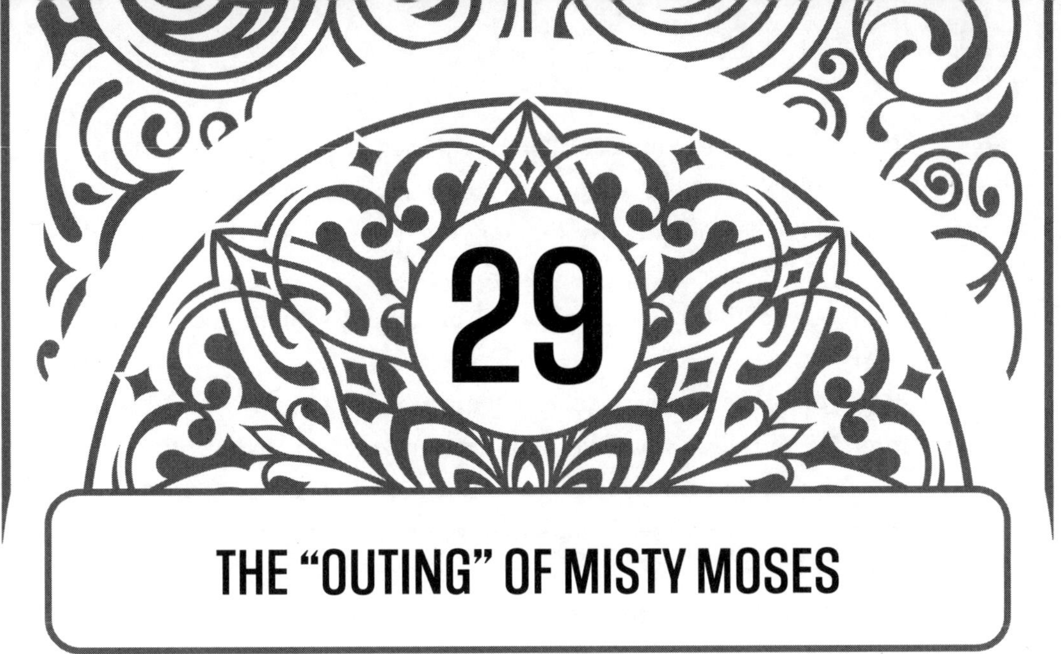

29

THE "OUTING" OF MISTY MOSES

PRESENT DAY

—OMG Dad! Have you been following all of this crazy renewed interest in Gigi's murder?

Frances Fletcher was texting with her father early one morning while jogging on her treadmill.

—No, sweetie. What do you mean?

Flynn Fletcher was feigning ignorance with his daughter. He had been following the social media hype regarding Misty Moses religiously, particularly Mystic Val's Instagram. He thought Valentina was an absolute idiot, but he still followed her constantly. He never liked Valentina, and she never liked him. But, as he often said, keep your friends close and your enemies even closer. Valentina probably had no clue that he was a follower of hers on Instagram. He used a fake name, of course: Buck Trevino. And, of course, Valentina allegedly had five million followers. Buck Trevino was just one of her millions of followers—both real and fake.

—Omg Dad. You're so out of it. There's this new theory that Misty Moses killed Gigi. MISTY MOSES!!! People are looking for her. It's like an all-out woman hunt! Lol. Wasn't she working for you at one time at that janitorial company you have? Her and her weirdo brother?

—Yeah. Actually, they both still are. You think I should be concerned about Misty?

—IDK. You're the lawyer, Dad! LOL. I mean, I don't know where this all came from. Do you think you have an obligation to report to the police that she works for you? I would assume you would know the answer to that.

—Well, are the police really looking for her or is this just some kind of crazy internet hoax? It's not like I am harboring a known fugitive if this is just some internet hoax and she's not wanted by law enforcement. She hasn't said anything to me about it—I mean, not that she necessarily would.

—Well, it all seems legit to me.

—Why does it seem legit? What are your sources on this?

—Well, it's everywhere. It's all over the internet. And Valentina is talking about it constantly on her social media.

—Good God. Just because it's all over the internet doesn't mean it's legitimate. People on the internet say that the earth is flat, and Elvis is alive. And Valentina is definitely not a reliable source. She's an idiot. Probably just trying to drum up something to throw people off her own trail. I have always thought Valentina was the one who killed Gigi. She got off scot-free and inherited the Mesero empire all to herself. Sold it off for a gazillion dollars before she had a chance to run it into the ground. She probably burned any evidence of the murder in that fire.

—Oh, Dad. I can't believe you still believe all that.

—I can't believe you don't think Valentina did it. Who had more motive than her? And she's the one who found Gigi's body. Her and that loser ex-husband of hers.

—We are just going to have to agree to disagree still on this one. I have always felt sorry for Valentina. And, besides, I know what it feels like for people to suspect you. Remember, I was named as a beneficiary in Gigi's life insurance policy. The cops questioned me relentlessly for a while because of that.

—Not like they did me, sweetie. You know, I'm the evil, corrupt ex-husband.

—Lol. Okay. Gtg. But do a Google search about Misty Moses and figure out what you should do. You are going to be shocked. It's just crazy. I'm beginning to think the theory might have legs to it. Maybe the police dropped the ball in their investigation, and they finally realized it.

Flynn replied to his daughter with an eye roll emoji. Frances then eye-rolled back and followed it with a heart emoji.

Flynn Fletcher put down his phone and sipped some coffee. He chuckled to himself. He was not "going to be shocked," as his daughter had predicted. He was fully up to speed on the Misty Moses internet circus. In fact, he egged Mystic Val on every day with likes, thumbs-ups, and messages telling her she should "hunt Misty down." He hadn't clued her in yet as to where Misty could be found. He was still thinking about how to approach that one.

Coincidentally, about the time he stopped texting, his phone rang. It was Misty.

"Hey, boss. I woke up feeling like hell today. I don't know what it is, but I don't think I can make it in." Misty started coughing violently.

"I'm sorry to hear that, Misty. You do sound like hell, all right. Must be something going around. We'll muddle through without you. Hope you're better tomorrow." He hung up the phone.

Flynn sat at his desk quietly for a few moments clicking on a ballpoint pen. Should he alert Valentina as to Misty's whereabouts or not? Or maybe alert the Shreveport Police or the Dallas Police? Hell, maybe the FBI was involved in this lunacy by now. But Flynn didn't like cops. He decided he wasn't going to go that route. He'd send an anonymous message to Mystic Val. She'd be like a dog with a bone with this information.

"Buck Trevino" began typing to Mystic Val on one of his numerous burner phones in Flynn's desk drawer.

"Hey, Mystic Val, I have heard from a good source that Misty Moses now goes by the name Misty Darnell and lives in Shreveport, Louisiana. Check out the Magnolia Bend mobile home park just east of town. I know someone who works with her doing janitorial work at the Shreveport casinos. Says Misty is quiet and acts real suspicious all the time."

Six hours later Officer Dupree of the Shreveport Police Department was on the phone with Detective Gil Gilmore of the Dallas Police Department.

"Hey, what's up, Gil? How's the Misty Moses investigation going? Are you going to be coming over to Shreveport any time soon?"

"Well, that's what I'm calling you about. Our investigative team still thinks this is a bunch of bullshit that the internet conspiracy theorists have come up with. Or maybe we even have some sort of deep fake going on, where someone—the real killer—is joining into all this hoopla to throw everybody off and set Misty up. It's just infuriating to those of us who have worked so hard on this. It's not like we didn't work this and every other possible angle to death. But nevertheless, I'm going to ask a favor."

"Sure. Anything, Gil. You name it."

"Well, believe it or not, I'd like you to go do a welfare check on Misty. We've been monitoring the web chat about her today—like we've been doing during all of this—and suddenly your Misty Darnell has been outed today."

"What do you mean?"

"Gigi Mesero's sister is now a social media influencer who goes by the name Mystic Val. She's really taken up the charge on the whole Misty Moses conspiracy. Even more than any of those true crime podcasters. And one of her followers today posted the address for Misty Darnell in Shreveport and said it's the Misty Moses that everyone has been looking for. Mystic Val and her followers are going crazy over it. They're probably going to head out to her place with torches and pitchforks. I'm frankly worried about the woman's safety."

"Wow. Just when you thought this couldn't get any crazier. But, sure. Why don't I run by the business she works for first and try to catch her before she heads home tonight? Maybe encourage her to find somewhere else to stay for a while."

"Well, here's the thing. I actually made an anonymous call earlier to that business you told me she works at, asking to speak with her, and I was told she was out sick today."

"Okay. Well, I don't know if that's good or bad. But I'll head out to her trailer park ASAP."

Thirty minutes later, Officer Dupree was knocking on Misty's door at the Magnolia Bend mobile home park. No answer. He knocked again. Still no answer. He noticed her dusty silver Toyota sedan out front. She was likely asleep or sick in bed and didn't want to get up. Officer Dupree decided to walk around the trailer and peek in some windows. He found one with torn venetian blinds that were partially drawn. He could view into a bedroom through that window. Inside, he saw Misty lying stiff, with her face tilted to the side away from the window. It was a little dark and hard to see. He peered closer. Shit. He could see blood on the pillow. And both blood and a bluish-green liquid were dripping from her mouth. There was a bottle of NyQuil on the bed stand next to her.

"Holy shit!"

Officer Dupree immediately called his sergeant for police backup and for EMTs. "Sarge, I need assistance ASAP. I was doing a welfare check over here at the Magnolia Bend mobile home park. Dallas police requested it. It's related to one of their investigations. But I think I may have found the woman that they wanted me to check on dead inside her trailer. And I have reason to believe it may not be natural causes. I can't get a great look inside the window, but I think I can see blood on the pillow and maybe some coming out of her mouth. I need both EMTs and probably crime scene processors."

"Jesus. I'm coming over and we'll have backup ASAP. Hang on a minute."

Officer Dupree could hear the sergeant giving commands and getting assistance. He returned to the phone. "Have you tried to make entry?"

"No, I just knocked a lot on the door. It was just a welfare check. I, of course, don't have a warrant. Am I able to go inside?"

"Well, EMTs will be there in a few minutes. Look through that window and announce yourself again. See if you can get a closer look."

Officer Dupree peered through the window again. Was she for sure dead? Maybe not. Maybe she was just passed out, sick or drowsy on cold medicine. Maybe she was coughing up blood. If so, he should immediately break in to try to help her and not wait for the EMTs.

"Ma'am. Ms. Moses. Officer Dupree from the Shreveport Police. Can you hear me? Are you okay? Ms. Moses? *Ms. Moses?*"

Officer Dupree backed away from the window. "Shit, I don't know, Sarge. I think she's dead. And if this is a crime scene, I'm afraid I've left my own footprints all over the place. What was I thinking? I've possibly trampled all over evidence."

By this time, the sergeant was in his car speeding to the trailer park. "You need to calm down, Dupree. Next time, you need to go with a second officer on a welfare call. Just keep by the window now and quit walking around. Just wait. The cavalry will be there soon."

Officer Dupree stepped forward again and looked more intently through the window. Shit. Misty was definitely dead. No doubt. It looked like rigor mortis had set in. He began to take some pictures of her through the window, just in case he needed them. As he did, he noticed for the first time a white sheet of paper on her large abdomen. What was that? Strange.

The EMTs arrived first, in about five minutes. Officer Dupree pointed through the window. "I'm pretty sure she's dead. Stiff as a board. Blood is on the pillow, and something blue is coming out of her mouth. Probably the NyQuil sitting on the table next to her. There may also be blood coming out of her mouth. We've got to be cautious and treat this as a possible crime scene. Crime scene investigators and my sarge will be here any second."

One of the EMTs looked at Officer Dupree strangely. "I heard you were just here on a welfare check. Not sure why you suspect foul play, Officer. She looks like an obese woman. My guess is she may have been over-self-medicating some respiratory problems with NyQuil when she probably should have seen a doctor. See it a lot."

"Please trust me on this and treat it as a possible crime scene. I was out here because we were requested to do a welfare check on her by law enforcement officers in Texas. They thought she might be in danger. She has been suspected in an old murder case, and there was internet chatter from people who wanted to come here and confront her over that."

An hour later, the EMTs had left, a medical examiner had arrived, and the investigation team had finished their job.

Officer Dupree looked at them with an expectant face when they finally emerged from the trailer. “Well?”

“Looks like it was a suicide, buddy. Gunshot through the mouth. Ruger twenty-two-caliber revolver. Only her prints on it, and she left a note. I can’t share the details of her note right now, but it’s a bombshell. You’ll know soon enough.”

30

SUICIDE?

PRESENT DAY

The curious case of Misty Moses Darnell got even more curious. In a few days, word got out that she had been found dead in Shreveport in her trailer, gunshot wound to the head with a suicide note on her body. In a twist of irony—or, perhaps, an intentional gesture—she had also ingested a large amount of NyQuil. It had not been laced with strychnine. She just ingested a lot of it, perhaps to relax herself before her final act.

The big reveal was the suicide note she left. In all capital letters and in blue ink, she allegedly wrote:

I DID IT. I KILLED GIGI MESERO. SHE HATED ME AND I HATED HER. I'M TIRED OF LIVING WITH IT.

Avery threw down the Sunday *Dallas Morning News* on the kitchen table with a heavy sigh. She shook her head and made herself a second cup of coffee. The paper contained extended weekend coverage regarding the "shocking breakthrough" in the long, unsolved Gigi Mesero murder case. The story recounted the details of Gigi's strychnine poisoning on that chilly December night at the Mystic Spires penthouse; the colorful and tragic history of the landmark hotel—with all its quirky guests, scandals, and fires over the years; the storied life and times of Gigi's elegant, immigrant parents, Guillermo and Vivienne (aka the "Lioness") Mesero; all the different suspects that there had been in the murder investigation; and now, finally, an answer to the who-dunit. The murderess had shockingly been a former hotel housekeeper with a grudge. Gigi had fired her. Misty Moses Darnell was a person whose name was never mentioned as a suspect. It was not until sleuths on the internet, including Gigi's grieving sister, began investigating Misty and raising the possibility that police had overlooked her that her identity had come to light. The internet and technology had literally solved this crime. Case closed.

Avery looked over at Max. "Well?"

"Well, what?"

"Do you believe a word of this?"

"I knew that's what you meant."

"Well, do you?"

"Nope."

"That's all you have to say? Nope?"

"I don't know what else to say. I barely touched this case. One night for two or three hours. But I don't think Misty did it."

"So, you think her suicide was staged? Or what?"

"Well, I guess I do. Yeah."

"So, what are you going to do?"

"What do you mean what am I going to do?"

"It can't just all end this way."

"It can and it has. We can't do anything about this. Some of us will always have our doubts. But it is what it is. Misty's death was ruled a suicide. She left a suicide note confessing. Case closed. It won't be the first time someone got away with murder. I mean, assuming that's what happened here."

"Well, you always said a woman did it. Poison is a weapon of choice of a woman typically. Not a man."

"Yep."

"You still think Valentina did it, don't you."

"Yep."

"I can't believe Valentina did it. I just can't believe a woman would kill her sister. They were all they had in the world. No parents. No children. No other siblings. And no jury will ever get to hear all the evidence and decide. I am literally distraught over this."

"So, who do you think did it, Avery?"

"Flynn Fletcher. He killed Gigi so she wouldn't be able to testify against him in his upcoming trials. And he staged Gigi's death to make it look like a woman did it. He was hoping Valentina would get framed. And once Misty became a suspect on the internet, he smelled opportunity. He could frame Misty for it and kill her and stage her death as a suicide. She was working for him! What are the odds of that?"

"I don't know, Avery. Maybe you're right, but it doesn't matter. It's over."

31

THE SWENSONS

PRESENT DAY

Maddie and Tanner Swenson were quietly sitting at a table having breakfast at the Bluebonnet Café. It was one of those small-town cafés where half the people knew each other, and the other half were people just traveling through town. It had an old-timey jukebox and had the best homemade pies in Texas.

Maddie stood up. "I'm going to go over to the pie counter and order a couple to take with us when we leave. Ask the waitress to pour me some more coffee when she comes by, would you?"

"You bet." Tanner was reading the morning paper. He stopped and watched Maddie walk away. He then pulled out some change from his pocket and flipped through the selections on the jukebox. He found "Brown Eyed Girl" by Van Morrison, put his change in the box, and selected the song. As Maddie headed back to the table a couple of moments later, she recognized the song and knew Tanner had selected it.

Maddie sat back down. She waved the waitress down for more coffee. Tanner had already forgotten he was supposed to do that.

"So I see you've been reading all those articles in the paper about Gigi. I can't even stand to read them. I can't believe you can."

Tanner shrugged his shoulders. "It's been a few years now. It's high time that they arrested someone for her murder. Can't believe the way it all came about."

"What do you mean?"

"Well, apparently this woman Misty Moses wasn't ever a suspect—or at least not a serious suspect. Then out of the blue she gets outed on the internet, and it's like these true crime podcasters put it all together. And Valentina gets involved, too. Then, bam. Misty Moses commits suicide in a Shreveport mobile home park. And confesses. It's just crazy. Hard to believe it could be as simple as all that."

"Yeah. Kind of hard to believe."

Maddie finally got the attention of the waitress, who freshened her coffee.

Tanner stirred his pancakes in some maple syrup. "She was a special lady, wasn't she."

"Yeah, she was. I miss her. We always had such fun with her when she came out to the ranch. Would have been great if she had bought that property she was looking at and started getting more involved with horses like she always wanted to do."

Tanner looked back at Maddie like he wasn't sure he believed her.

"So what kind of pies did you order?"

"One cherry and one peanut butter."

32

PAYBACK?

PRESENT DAY

Ivy Fletcher Stevens was a single mom who worked as a paralegal and yoga instructor in Austin, Texas. She was Flynn Fletcher's younger sister (his only sibling). The two were not terribly close but not estranged either. They just had totally separate interests and lives. Occasionally Flynn's daughter, Frances, would visit her Aunt Ivy and Ivy's two young kids. Ivy had barely gotten to know Gigi during her and Flynn's brief marriage.

One night, as Ivy was locking up her yoga studio in a strip shopping center in West Austin, after dark, when no one was around, two armed men in ski masks and dark clothes grabbed her and stuffed her into the trunk of a rented sedan that they were driving. They tied up her hands and gagged her. They sped out to a deserted area in the Hill Country approaching Dripping Springs. When they got to a turnoff near US 290 and SH 21 that was sufficiently secluded, they pulled over, got out of the car, and opened the trunk. They yanked Ivy out of the trunk. They then called up Aldo Moses in Shreveport, Louisiana. They used FaceTime.

When Aldo answered his phone, they pointed the phone toward Ivy. One of the men said, "Tell this man on the phone what your name is. It could be a matter of life and death. Your life and death."

Ivy squirmed and cried. "Who are you? Why are you doing this to me? I'm a mother of two small kids. I'm all they have!"

"We know you have kids. Maybe they're next if you don't cooperate. Tell us your name."

"It's Ivy. Ivy Stevens."

"Are you Flynn Fletcher's sister?"

"Yes. Why?"

The two men looked at Aldo Moses. "Well? We've followed your instructions. Do you want us to go through with it?"

Aldo responded, "Kill her. Make a video of it and text it to this number." He then gave the men Flynn Fletcher's phone number.

Aldo then, before hanging up, said, "Ivy Fletcher, your brother killed my sister. He framed her for something she didn't do. This is payback. Plain and simple. I'm sorry for your sake you have such a scum brother." And then he hung up.

Ivy Fletcher Stevens's body, killed with one gunshot to the head, was left abandoned on the side of a country road. Her murder would go unsolved. There were no witnesses. No suspects. She had no enemies. She lived a quiet life. It was believed to simply be a random act of violence. Just another statistic of a pretty young woman being abducted and murdered. When it was reported by news outlets, no one even mentioned that she was Flynn Fletcher's sister.

Six weeks later, the Flamethrower and Aldo Moses apparently made amends and let bygones be bygones. The Flamethrower came out of retirement from practicing law to file a lawsuit for Aldo Moses against a well-known open-source AI platform and its search engine parent company. The theory of the case: Misty Moses had been encouraged to commit suicide after discussing it at length with the defendant, the AI platform, and it egged her on and bolstered her resolve to do it. The lawsuit explained that Misty had a "significant history of trauma" and experienced psychotic episodes. The lawsuit further argued that AI platforms such as the defendant "lack appropriate guardrails to prevent inappropriate interactions"—in particular, when it comes to mentally troubled people. The plaintiff, Aldo Moses, argued that his sister Misty would not have died her terrible death by suicide if not for her extensive conversations with the AI platform. The Flamethrower sought a whopping $100 million in damages and took on the representation for Aldo on a typical one-third contingency fee basis. It would be interesting to see how he argued for $100 million of damages, considering that Misty had confessed to a murder, had no children, and was generally not a very sympathetic victim, to say the least. Of course, every good lawyer knows that when you don't have good facts, you argue the law, and when you don't have good law, you argue the facts. If you have neither good facts nor good law, you obfuscate. The Flamethrower was pretty good at obfuscation, so it was anyone's guess how this lawsuit might turn out.

33

SALAMANCA

"So why did you choose Salamanca for our lunch today, Avery? Is it because it reminds you of Spain, which you love so much, or is it because it's across the street from where the Mystic Spires used to be—which you still obsess over so much?"

Avery was having a Saturday afternoon lunch at a trendy new tapas bar with Suzanne, Julia, and Kat.

"Maybe it's just because I just like their tapas here so much, Suzanne. And their sangria, of course." Avery touched her wineglass with Suzanne's and said, "Cheers."

Julia spoke up. "It's both things you said, Aunt Suzanne. Spain and Mystic Spires. Mom is definitely still obsessing over Mystic Spires and Gigi Mesero."

Avery swirled her drink. "Guilty as charged."

Julia replied, "And yet she criticizes me for following Mystic Val on social media. Does that make any sense?"

"I criticize you, Julia, for wasting your precious time and brain space on vacuous, talentless social media influencers. People who contribute nothing of value to society. People who are fake and vain and earn money for doing nothing."

"Ouch! Tell us how you really feel, Avery. You're making me feel guilty, because I follow Mystic Val, too."

"I know you do, Suzanne. Julia has told me."

"Is it really just Mystic Val that you have a problem with, Avery, or is it social influencers generally? Is it just that you think that Valentina is the one who killed Gigi and she's gotten away with it?"

"It's social media influencers generally. But, no, there's no way I think Valentina killed her sister! Surely, Suzanne, your brain can't go there either!"

"Well, Avery, I mean, not everyone loves their sister the way we love each other. So, I can imagine it happening in theory. But I don't think Valentina killed Gigi. Why are we even having this conversation? Isn't it settled? Misty Moses killed Gigi. She confessed and committed suicide. Case closed."

"Well, case closed, yes. But will I ever be convinced? No."

"Well, who do you think did it? I've always thought it was that cowboy's wife. Maddie Swenson."

"Maybe. That's probably a better theory than Misty Moses. But I always thought it had to be Flynn Fletcher. The Flamethrower. Even though Max says men don't use poison to kill. It's a woman's weapon of choice. I still think the Flamethrower did it. He had the greatest motive. He was a sleazebag. He was corrupt. He framed Misty when he saw the opportunity."

"And he went by the nickname the Flamethrower. Anyone who picks such a stupid nickname has to be guilty, right?" Kat commented with a grin.

"Avery, does Max think Misty did it?"

"Nope. He thinks it was Valentina."

"Well, I guess we will never know."

"I guess. It won't be the first time a woman dies, and justice is never done. Happens all the time."

"Avery, if you are so disillusioned with our justice system, what does that say? I mean, you're a judge, and you're married to a cop."

"Retired."

"Retired cop."

"I'm not really disillusioned with our legal system. It's still the best human beings can muster. It's the nonhumans that I'm worried about. The

AI. And I am also worried about people losing faith in our legal system. Losing faith in all our institutions really."

"What does that mean, Mom?"

"I'm just saying I don't think there is any way that law enforcement overlooked Misty. I think they were passionate and thorough in their investigation. Day and night, with great care and competence. But for some whacky reason, those AI platforms decided that Misty could be a suspect. They are just machines. Computer algorithms that have never been trained in law and have no intuition or judgment. And they aren't duty bound to bear allegiance to the Constitution. They probably just matched data points, like where she lived—in other words, that she was in close proximity to the crime, so she had opportunity. Also, the data point that she worked at the Mystic Spires and was terminated shortly before the murder. Also, that she had a boyfriend that was a criminal. Maybe one or two other bits of circumstantial evidence were generated. And guess what? That was probably all considered by the police, too."

"And then I guess when your law clerk group started searching Misty Moses on social media and reaching out about her on crime blogs and with the true crime podcasters, suddenly the power of the internet and social media kicked in. The Misty Moses theory went viral, as the saying goes."

"Yep. You got it, Suzanne. And what may have been only minor, passing interest in the subject by a few was pumped up through fake likes and fake thumbs-ups, and probably even some fake comments by fake followers. The smoke and mirrors of the internet. It looked like there was far more interest in the subject than there probably really was."

"Bots?"

"Well, maybe bots and maybe click-farm workers in some faraway country with cheap labor."

"Oh no. Here Mom goes. She is about to give a lecture about click farms again. Her new favorite subject. Two years ago, Bitcoin was her favorite subject. Now click farms."

Kat chimed in. "What's a click farm?"

Julia moaned. "No! You had to ask. This is going to turn into a thirty-minute discussion."

Avery frowned at her daughter. "I'll spare you, Kat. Suffice it to say that when a person has a gazillion followers or a gazillion reviews or likes on a product, don't be gullible and assume it's true. Many people and companies out there are taking advantage of opportunities to fool the public. And the public is complicit by believing it without investigation. Be skeptical. Don't fall for everything that's out there. It's getting harder and harder to discern real versus fake."

Suzanne looked concerned. "Avery, please don't tell me you're becoming one of those people who think that the internet and technology are ruining society. I mean, think about how much better it's made our lives in so many ways."

"No, that's not what I am saying. I'm just afraid of us getting to the point where we forget how to think. Forget how to reason. We are just lemmings staring at a screen. And what's on the screen is sometimes toxic or even dangerous."

"People, of course, said that about TV. And probably radio before that."

"Yeah, but somehow our government figured out how to regulate those things appropriately. The government has been way behind on this. Hopelessly behind. Anyway, that's all way above my pay grade. But I do know something about how the legal system is supposed to work. And I always say that the internet is easy. But a courtroom is hard. We make people put on reliable evidence and prove their case before decisions are made or verdicts are rendered. The jury system permits people to see actual humans take a witness stand, just a few feet away from them, and assess whether they seem believable. The jury has to go back in a room and talk about it all, face-to-face. If they get it wrong, then there are ways to appeal and challenge that. But meanwhile, Mystic Val, with her allegedly millions of followers, can announce that she believes Misty Moses killed her sister, and, next thing you know, society believes it's true. The power of the internet is bigger than anything humankind has ever experienced. It can be used to destroy people like nothing else I can think of."

The girls by this time were glued to their phones.

"Avery, Misty did confess in a suicide note. Do you not believe that? Do you think it was staged?"

"Yes, I do. It's just my gut."

"Well, what's worse? A machine that has no gut? No intuition? Or a human whose gut is sometimes wrong? Who is sometimes biased, perhaps?"

"They are both wrong. It's why we have a system designed so that evidence prevails, and in criminal cases, it needs to be evidence that is beyond a reasonable doubt. I mean, we have rules of evidence that have been developed over hundreds of years to hopefully increase reliability and fairness. And, while humans make mistakes, at least we have a process to correct those mistakes. Objections. Appeals. Layers of people involved in the process."

They all sat in silence for a few moments. The conversation had gotten a little heavy for a Saturday afternoon—especially since sangria was involved. Meanwhile, at a table nearby, a woman was taking pictures of her food, then having her boyfriend video her talking about her food and drink. The bubbly young woman was dressed in colorful, fashionable clothes with perfect fake hair, fake fancy jewelry, long false eyelashes, and long, fake red nails.

Avery spoke up. "Let me guess. A social influencer?"

Julia responded. "Yes. And you can just say 'influencer,' Mom."

"Oh. Excuse me. I don't want to get the lingo wrong. But really, why does she think people care about what she is eating or drinking? Is this just advertising, plain and simple, and the public doesn't recognize it for what it is?"

Suzanne replied, "I don't know, but you've got to see this. Mystic Val's newest posts. She's gone blond. Says she needed a drastic change now that she is in this new chapter of her life after Gigi's killer has finally been identified. And look at her face. I can't figure out if it's extensive plastic surgery or filtering or what. She looks completely different."

Kat leaned over to her mother's phone. "I think that's just a good filter, Mom."

"I tell you everything is fake these days. Only dogs are real. When dogs start becoming fake, I'm out. Finished." Avery looked out in the distance.

"Mom, there have been robot dogs for years now. Hello?"

"Oh, look," Kat continued. "Val is going to have her own cryptocurrency soon that she's coming out with. It's going to be called Mystocoin. She's hired a team of creators and miners that were previously pioneers of Bitcoin and there's going to be a big public announcement soon."

Avery shook her head. "Oh, good. I bet that's going to work out well. Are y'all ready to order? Why didn't they bring us menus, I wonder?"

"Mom. Nobody has menus anymore. There's a QR code on the table. Use your phone!"

"Of course. What was I thinking? I need more sangria. Suzanne, what about you?"

34

LEGAL PLAYBOOKS

PRESENT DAY

"Judge, why are lawyers so predictable? And why are clients so predictable? It's like they all have the very same playbook. They can't vary from it ever."

Millicent had just walked into Judge Lassiter's chambers office on a day that they didn't have court. Judge Lassiter had brought Jake and Finley to work, and they were snoring on her couch.

Avery looked at Millicent and sipped on her second cup of coffee. "Milly, is that just a rhetorical question or one that you really expect me to answer for you?"

"I don't know. I'm just frustrated, Judge." Milly plopped down on the couch next to the dogs. They barely moved, but Jake opened one eye as if annoyed by the disturbance. The dogs had taken to commandeering this courthouse couch as their own during their visits.

"Well, speaking of frustration, how's your drafting of that opinion on the Oakmont Capital matter coming along? We are coming up on sixty days since we took the matter under advisement. Are we going to wind up on the slow-poke list?"

"Sorry, Judge. I admit that I'm like a tortoise at a computer lately. This opinion is so hard. And it's long. And it's about as interesting as an instruction manual for assembling a piece of IKEA furniture."

"How long is the opinion so far? You remember my measuring stick on these things, right?"

"I know. I know. If the opinion is longer than Ernest Hemingway's *The Old Man and the Sea*, it's too long. Personally, I think that's rather arbitrary, Judge. *The Old Man and the Sea* is considered a novella, not a novel. It was only like twenty-nine thousand words long."

"Yes, and yet it won the Pulitzer Prize. Brevity is a good thing. I need my law clerks to be Hemingway, not Faulkner. Anyway, please wrap it up by Friday. Send me whatever you have. But back to your question. Why were you bemoaning lawyers and clients having legal playbooks? What prompted that epiphany?"

"I don't know. I guess it's just starting to feel like, the longer I do this, that lawyers aren't really as creative and clever as they like to think that they are—as I thought they would be when I was in my law school days."

"Well, not every case has interesting facts or cutting-edge law. And it's not the lawyers' job to entertain us."

"I know, Judge. That's not what I'm getting at. It's just like there are fact patterns we see again and again and there seems to be a template that every lawyer follows every single time. It's no wonder that experts predict lawyers will eventually be replaced by AI."

"Okay, Milly. Tell me what you mean."

"Well, in every commercial civil dispute, we have these alphabet-soup companies. Companies with names like LTR, LLC vs. BRNDT, L.P., and they have affiliates with almost identical names like LTR, Inc. and LTR Holdings and LTR International and LTR II, Inc. and LTR, III, Inc. and so on."

"Millicent, I'll stop you right there. It's not the goal of lawyers to torture judges and their law clerks with these alphabet-soup names that are impossible to keep straight. It's just that corporate lawyers are the least creative human beings on the planet. They are the ones responsible for the alphabet-soup names and they apparently never think about how confusing it's going to be down the road if there's ever a lawsuit. God forbid they come up with names that are snappy or descriptive or at least easy to keep straight.

And the vast web of entities that they always create—if that's where you are going next—that's usually about isolating liabilities within companies so that an entire corporate enterprise doesn't become liable and collapse if, say, one product line or business line gets exposed to a lawsuit. And it's also about taking advantage of tax laws, so you can thank your congressmen and women for that."

"I suppose you are going to tell me that the same holds true for the vast number of offshore companies that the lawyers so often create and the web of umpteen bank accounts?"

"Well, yes, tax savings. And achieving efficient cash management."

"So, are you telling me I'm just cynical to think it's all about obfuscating and hiding assets from future plaintiffs' lawyers and the government?"

Avery giggled. "Well, dear Milly, we have to judge each situation differently, but your theory is often correct. It's sometimes about obfuscation. Sometimes, the obfuscators might argue that they are just legitimately protecting their assets from unknown claims that might pop up in the future. From so-called 'existential threats.' They are protecting their shareholders to whom they owe duties—protecting their value—or maybe even the company's lenders insisted on setting up separate structures."

Milly looked skeptical. "And speaking of lenders, I used to think a lender was a bank. It feels like we rarely see banks in court anymore. All of the lenders seem to be hedge funds and private equity companies or other alternative lenders who sometimes seem to have been willing to loan money to anybody for the right amount of fees and interest. Then, they flip the loans like hot potatoes to some other unsuspecting assignee of the lender. Who later flips to someone else. Then the company defaults on the loan and the lender that is now holding the loan expresses shock and dismay."

Avery laughed. "And what is the lender's playbook, Milly? Do you think they have playbooks, too?"

"Oh, different playbooks. But yes, playbooks. They scream fraud a lot. They want you to punish the company for borrowing the money, saying things like the company lied and induced the lender to make the loan with false pretenses, the owners used funds like their own personal piggy bank, assets have disappeared, and the company was running a shell game with a complex web of accounts. Oh, and that the company frivolously bought a private jet. Which, I might add, companies in our court always seem to have purchased private jets. Ridiculous, if you ask me."

"Oh, I might buy a private jet if I could afford one. Don't forget about the never-ending allegations of document shredding and hard-drive scrubbing and missing phones."

Tom walked in.

Avery looked up. "Oh, come on, Tom. That's not always in the playbook. A lot of times, sure. But not always."

Tom was more cynical than Millicent. "And then it gets really fun when the lender convinces the FBI that someone at the company committed wire fraud or bank fraud. It's all pretty much fun and games until the guys in windbreakers show up at the door seizing boxes and computers. Pretty much a foregone conclusion at that point that someone is going to be taking a flight to the UAE or some other foreign country with no extradition treaty with the U.S."

"Oh my God, you two! Your young idealism has so quickly turned to jaded dismay. Our business disputes are not all as sleazy as you make it sound. We have some really good people and companies and lenders involved many times who are just trying to make the world a better place with their products and services. Sometimes they face hard times."

"Is this the part where you tell us that there are truly some 'corporate Bambis,' Judge?"

"We've just had a bad run of cases lately with some scandalous facts. Tom, did you have something to ask me? I thought you were supposed to be tied up with training this morning."

"Well, I was, but the security guards just told me to tell you that there's a guy who wandered in the courtroom who said he wants to see you and wants to ask for a continuance of an upcoming hearing."

"Well, please just go out and tell him that's not how we do things. He can't just wander in like we're a fast-food restaurant and expect to see the judge without a noticed hearing."

"Yes, but he's pro se and looks to be in pretty bad shape."

"How so?"

"His head is all wrapped up in a bandage roll, like a mummy, with only a small amount of his face showing. And there's a cord coming out of the top of his head, also wrapped in bandages, and the cord leads to some sort of canvas bag that he is holding. And there's some blood on the bandages."

"Oh my God," Millicent squeaked, and the dogs jumped. "This is a new page in the playbook I haven't seen before. Should we call the marshals? Or 911?"

Avery went to the closet to grab her robe. "Good grief. Let's go out in the courtroom and see what we have here. I'm guessing this is a guy suddenly and coincidentally having a health issue just when it's time to go to trial—definitely part of the playbook—but this I have got to see. Never had the whole mummy presentation thing before. I have had lots of neck braces and plaster of paris casts and wheelchairs, and even a guy in an iron lung once. But this sounds like it could be Academy Award–worthy. Please go get David to keep order in the courtroom and make a record."

As soon as David came up, Avery and the law clerks went into the courtroom. David did his usual formal "all rise" cry, even though it was only the bandaged-wrapped man in the courtroom. Avery began the impromptu hearing.

"Sir, if you are physically able, will you approach the podium and tell me your name?"

The man walked forward without any apparent difficulty. "I am Dr. Phil Raymond."

"Okay, Dr. Raymond. My law clerk said you are involved in a case that is set for trial soon, and you wanted to ask for a continuance. Normally, we would have told you to file a motion, but here you are, looking pretty bad, and you don't have a lawyer. So, I'll give you a moment to tell me your case name and what's going on. I'll decide if we need to try to get the other side on the phone."

For the next few minutes, the mummy-like man described his situation. He was having some vague neurological problems. He was being monitored by doctors. He, himself, was a doctor. His wife was divorcing him and engaged in a mission on social media to ruin him. He wanted all of his divorce matters heard by Judge Lassiter before she commenced the trial in his business case. He had heard from a friend that she could do that.

"Sir, you need to seek legal advice from a lawyer, not a friend. Have you tried to engage a lawyer?" As Avery waited for his answer, she pulled up the man's case file on her computer. The man had hired and fired five different law firms during his case. Never a good sign.

"I'm talking to several lawyers now about substituting into my case. They all are asking for retainers I cannot afford."

Avery scanned through the schedule of assets that the man had filed with the court. He had a large home, a vacation home, and also owned the real property on which his medical practice operated. He owned a Bentley automobile, a Porsche, a Land Rover, and a Maserati. He had lots of malpractice claims against him. He also showed that he earned income working as a medical expert for personal injury lawyers, including one "Flynn Fletcher." It showed Flynn Fletcher owed him a very large receivable. Good grief! Just when Avery least expected it, she was once again reminded of Gigi Mesero.

Avery cleared her throat. "Sir, if you file a motion for continuance with a doctor's note explaining the bandages, and if you have a new lawyer lined up, I will consider giving you a short continuance on your trial coming up, but this is not how we usually do things. We cannot have hearings like this with other parties in interest not here to express their views. And there is no way that I can or will take jurisdiction of your divorce case. That's not going to happen."

The mummy man stared at her in silence.

"Sir, are you hearing me?"

"Yes. I'll have a new lawyer lined up by tomorrow."

Avery hoped it wouldn't be Flynn Fletcher.

35

SMOKE AND MIRRORS AND LAWSUITS

PRESENT DAY

Flynn Fletcher, the Flamethrower, never strayed too far from his early career in the law. Sure, he dabbled in real estate development and tried his luck as a Texas lobbyist for a while. He solicited money from elderly investors once for a wind turbine farm that never materialized. He stayed one step ahead of the SEC on unscrupulous forays into sales of unregistered securities and somehow avoided an indictment. He owned businesses in Louisiana providing goods and services to casinos. But around the time he married Gigi, he started gravitating back to his legal roots and venturing into "third-party litigation funding" in the mass torts arena.

Mass torts litigation, of course, refers to high-volume personal injury or wrongful-death lawsuits involving an injurious product or a harm-producing event (e.g., opioids, Roundup weed killer, Camp Lejeune water contamination, etc.). Mass tort litigation is expensive for plaintiffs' lawyers—as the Flamethrower knew very well from his days practicing as a scrappy personal injury lawyer in New Jersey. Such lawyers often do not have the resources to go toe-to-toe with the prominent lawyers hired by the huge corporate defendants they are suing. This was one reason why the Flamethrower never progressed very far in his legal career beyond being a "slip-and-fall" attorney, suing casinos in his early days. In response to this imbalance of resources between financially challenged plaintiffs and deep-pocket defendants, third-party financing companies emerged to essentially be passive investors in the litigation—silent funders on the sidelines that have stockpiles of cash they need to deploy. Saviors, some think. But it's not that these funders feel sympathy for downtrodden plaintiffs. They, of course, are profit motivated. They provide capital to the plaintiffs' lawyers and get a share of the potentially massive contingency fees the plaintiffs' law firms eventually realize. In theory, this works—from an ethical standpoint—as long as the litigation funders stay passive and the clients make the important decisions about their lawsuits (including when to settle). Some suggest that these litigation funders are anything but "passive" in reality. Perhaps some are and some aren't. As with anything in life, sometimes a few bad apples can taint perceptions.

When the Flamethrower entered into this litigation funding world, he approached it with his usual attitude of taking the concept to a higher level. Accordingly, he approached a whiz-bang financial advisor whom he knew to be well-connected to hedge funds: Blake Martin, aka the Finance Bro. Fletcher had met Martin at a racket ball club in the Uptown area of Dallas. It was the place where all the hedge fund portfolio managers played.

The two of them deduced over some Blanton's Bourbon one afternoon that the weak links in this promising area of litigation funding agreements were the lengthy process of the litigation (i.e., the delayed payout) and the "passive" investor aspect of it. The litigation funders needed to control things more. But this was all difficult since litigation could get bogged down for years. And nosy judges sometimes wanted to look at litigation funding agreements to make sure clients and their lawyers maintained full control of the trajectory of the lawsuits. So, the ultimate hedging strategy emerged when they put their heads together. The litigation funding companies could broaden their yields in this whole endeavor. They could simultaneously invest (through separately created subsidiary investment companies) in the stocks, bonds, and even the secured debt of the defendant companies—that is, the very companies against whom they were funding lawsuits. They could acquire substantial stakes in these companies. Then, they could put pressure on the boards of the defendant companies to settle the lawsuits. It would be a win-win. They'd be on both sides of the lawsuit. The plaintiffs and their lawyers would get great contingency recoveries (in which the litigation funding companies would share). And the affiliated companies that were buying economic stakes in the defendant companies could make a windfall, too, if they played things just right—such as by first "shorting" the stock of these companies, and then spreading rumors in the financial markets that the defendant companies had massive exposure in these lawsuits—that they were about to lose big in litigation, and might be on the brink of financial ruin. This would cause the investment companies to make a small fortune on their "short" positions when the stock of these companies then plummeted; then the investment companies would buy up more stocks and bonds in the companies when they fell in value as a result of these rampant rumors; then they could enjoy the rebound in the stocks' and bonds' values when the lawsuits were settled favorably, and the defendant companies returned to financial health.

If this were not perfect enough, the Flamethrower and Finance Bro figured out how to improve upon their strategy. They would help amass a class of plaintiffs occasionally when needed. For example, if there were rumors that something like, say, a weight loss drug was causing health problems, they might finance a massive marketing effort of certain plaintiffs' law firms—who would subcontract to "lead generators"—to go rustle up some potential plaintiff-clients by all sorts of means (TV commercials, mailings, websites, social media advertising, call centers, etc.). They would engage a reliable medical expert, a trusted doctor (a Dr. Phil Raymond, aka Mummy Man)—to confirm harm had occurred to the plaintiffs. One might say that Flynn Fletcher and Blake Martin took an originally laudable "access to justice" tool and twisted it into a money-making machine for investors in the shadows. Sure, sometimes meritorious claims get a recovery that they might truly deserve. But a lot of fraudulent claims would get swept into a payday, too.

Judge Lassiter was sitting in chambers one morning when her law clerk Tom wandered in with coffee and what looked like a hangover.

"Late night, Tom?"

Tom grinned. "Yeah, but not a real fun one. I was up looking at the Pearls case."

Pearls Elixirs was an established American company dating back to the 1800s that made, among other things, an over-the-counter cough medicine that had been on the market for decades. Pearls Elixirs had been hit with a massive number of tort lawsuits in recent years and eventually filed Chapter 11 under the weight of that. It was now floundering in Judge Lassiter's court, trying to find a way out of the turmoil. The Pearls cough medicine at the center of the litigation allegedly had an almost undetectable trace of some toxin in it that was similar in composition to strychnine. A few people had died—allegedly from taking the cough medicine—and others had allegedly suffered damage to the central nervous system and muscle atrophy. There was no conclusive evidence that the Pearls cough medicine had actually caused this. But the lawsuits against Pearls had proliferated, nonetheless. The Pearls bankruptcy case had been a contentious one, with eighty thousand claims filed by individuals who were allegedly harmed from taking the cough medicine. Three law firms were representing this massive group of plaintiffs.

"So, what's on your mind, Tom?"

"Well, I was reviewing the litigation funding agreements that you required the three main plaintiffs' law firms to submit to you—against their strong opposition, I might add. I noticed that the private equity fund that provided litigation funding to the plaintiffs was called Foggy Capital. And guess what? Foggy Capital's affiliate, a sister company called Foghorn Opportunities, LLP, is a major debt holder and also an equity holder of Pearls company. The Foggy people are on all sides of the negotiation table, you might say—cozied up with the tort claimants that Foggy is financing, who are wanting a massive distribution and threatening to liquidate Pearls if they don't get it—and, meanwhile, Foghorn is holding bonds and equity and arguing that Pearls should be saved and suggesting that the tort claimants should be paid with stock of the company as opposed to cash."

"Wow. And no party in interest has raised this as a conflict of interest or other problem?"

"Nope. Do you suppose no one has connected the dots yet, or is this just the way of the world now that we are all supposed to accept? The world of big-stakes litigation. Accept it, step in line, or you're an unsophisticated rube."

Avery ignored the biting commentary. "Who are the folks behind Foggy Capital, I wonder? Do we know that?"

"This is the moment you've been waiting for, whether you realize it or not. Their documents are signed by a guy whose name you might recognize: Blake Martin."

"Blake Martin? The Finance Bro who dated Gigi Mesero?"

"I assume it is the same one. Blake Martin died in late 2018, but the litigation funding agreements were signed in 2017."

"Wow. I am almost speechless. Is this an insane coincidence, or what? Here I go again. I'm going to start obsessing about Gigi all over again. It's like the forces in the universe keep calling me back to her."

"The coincidences don't stop there, Judge. Guess what other name I found in this document? The so-called "Litigation Monitor" that was established in the litigation funding agreement is none other than Flynn Fletcher."

"What? Gigi's loser ex-husband? How on earth did Blake Martin and Flynn Fletcher connect? This is crazy!"

"I don't know. But think about it. Gigi dies in December 2016, then these litigation funding agreements are signed a few months later in 2017. Her ex-husband and ex-boyfriend are teaming up in a business venture?"

"Do you suppose that they met at her funeral? Jeez. What a way to mix business with whatever."

"And what about the fact that this litigation happens to involve litigation over a cough syrup with an allegedly toxic substance in it?"

Avery and Tom sat in silence.

Tom broke the silence. "Well, Judge, should we just sit back and let the chips fall where they may, or should we be more proactive?"

"I think I want to ponder this, Tom. Usually, good lawyers bring these things to the forefront when they start to realize there may be a problem. But I want to think on it. Thanks, Tom."

Avery sat back in her chair and rubbed her eyes. It felt like sometimes in these high-stakes cases, the finance wizards were always playing chess while so many of their adversaries were playing checkers. But this was not just a questionable litigation funding arrangement with anonymous (or near-anonymous) capital behind it. This was not just a private equity fund that was arguably exercising too much control or acting as a puppet master.

Or was it?

Avery walked over to her window and stared over at the land where the Mystic Spires had once stood. Her stomach felt sick. Flynn Fletcher must have killed Gigi. Perhaps Blake Martin knew it or was part of it; perhaps not. Flynn Fletcher was thumbing his nose at the world with this concocted Pearls Elixirs litigation. He poisoned Gigi. This was his sick, cruel next chapter. It was, no doubt, funny to him. Irony. Poison in a cough syrup killed my ex-wife. And now I am making a fortune, financing plaintiffs' lawyers suing a Big American Company for poisoning the public with their cough syrup.

EPILOGUE

Maddie Swenson sat in her kitchen reading the morning paper. She saw a large advertisement:

> If you used Pearls Elixirs cough syrup between the years 2000 and 2020 and have subsequently developed muscle atrophy or damage to the central nervous system, you may be entitled to legal compensation. Experts have opined that a toxin detected in this product may be responsible for your injuries. You may be eligible to become a member of a class action lawsuit. Lawyers are standing by.

Other details and the lawyers' names to contact were listed below the advertisement. Flynn Fletcher was one of those names. Gigi's despicable ex.

Maddie giggled a bit. She wondered if NyQuil would soon be identified as also containing this same "toxin." What were the odds? Maybe someone would soon wonder if Gigi was not murdered after all?

Maddie closed her eyes and thought back to a few days before Christmas 2016, when she and Tanner went to Gigi's penthouse for Gigi's annual holiday party. Everything was so beautiful. Gigi was so beautiful. The Mystic Spires was lit up and decorated like a holiday wonderland. Gigi had lavish gifts for everyone. The food was exquisite. And Tanner could not take his eyes off of Gigi. He danced with Gigi, laughed with her, and walked out on the balcony with her—gazing up at the stars.

Maddie had to do it. She had to stop this nonsense. She walked back into Gigi's bedroom. She wondered how many times Tanner had been in this room. She sat on Gigi's big plush bed. She caressed the pillows. She looked around. She grabbed a pair of velvet gloves out of her black leather purse. She then pulled a bottle of NyQuil out of it. She put the bottle into Gigi's nightstand drawer. No one would ever know. The trace of strychnine was almost undetectable. It would look like, at worst, a suicide.

ABOUT THE AUTHOR

Stacey Jernigan, a native Texan, has been a judge in Dallas, Texas, since 2006. Before that, she was a lawyer and partner at a large international law firm, specializing in corporate restructuring matters. She is also an occasional adjunct professor at the SMU Dedman School of Law.

Stacey is married to a retired law enforcement officer (Dallas Police Department), with whom she has an adult son and daughter, as well as two Cavalier King Charles spaniels. She is a frequent speaker at legal conferences around the country and is an avid writer and international traveler. *Mystic Spires Post-Mortem* is her third novel.

In her free time, Stacey cheers for her favorite college sports teams from her two alma maters: the University of Texas Longhorns and the SMU Mustangs.